THE KNIGHT AND DEATH
THREE NOVELLAS

LEONARDO SCIASCIA was born in 1921 at Racalmuto, near Agrigento, in southwestern Sicily. He taught in a primary school, trained as a lawyer, and published his first novel, *The Day of the Owl*, in 1961. He also took an active part in politics, with a seat in parliament first as a Communist, later as a Radical. He died in 1989 leaving a rich and varied opus including novels, short stories and very trenchant reportage on his native Sicily. "Out of his curious Sicilian experience," writes Gore Vidal, "Sciascia made a literature that is not quite like anything else ever done by a European."

Other novels and stories by Sciascia to be issued in Harvill paperbacks include *The Council of Egypt*, *Death of an Inquisitor* and *Candido*.

Also by Leonardo Sciascia

SICILIAN UNCLES
THE DAY OF THE OWL
EQUAL DANGER
THE WINE-DARK SEA
ONE WAY OR ANOTHER
THE MYSTERY OF MAJORANA
THE MORO AFFAIR

Leonardo Sciascia

THE KNIGHT AND DEATH

THREE NOVELLAS

Translated from the Italian by
Joseph Farrell and Marie Evans

HARVILL
An Imprint of HarperCollinsPublishers

First published in Italy by Adelphi Edizioni, Milan, 1987–89
First published in Great Britain by Carcanet Press Ltd. 1991
This edition first published in 1992
by Harvill
an imprint of HarperCollins Publishers,
77/85 Fulham Palace Road,
Hammersmith, London W6 8JB

1 3 5 7 9 8 6 4 2

Il Cavaliere e la morte (sotie) © 1988 Adelphi Edizioni s.p.a. Milan;
Una storia semplice © 1989 Adelphi Edizioni s.p.a. Milan;
Porte aperte © 1987 Adelphi Edizioni s.p.a. Milan

Translations and essay © 1991 Joseph Farrell
Translation, preface & notes © 1991 Marie Evans

The rights of Joseph Farrell and Marie Evans to be identified as
the translators of these works have been asserted by them
in accordance with the Copyright, Designs and Patents Act of 1988.

A CIP catalogue record for this book is
available from the British Library.

ISBN 0 00 271291 1

Set in Linotron Bembo by
Servis Filmsetting Ltd, Manchester

Printed and bound in Great Britain by
HarperCollins Manufacturing, Glasgow

CONTENTS

The Knight and Death   7

A Straightforward Tale   75

Open Doors   123

Sciascia's Late Fiction   203

The Knight and Death

(a *sotie*)

TRANSLATED BY JOSEPH FARRELL

An old Danish bishop, I remember, once told me that there are many ways of reaching truth, and that burgundy is one of the many.

KAREN BLIXEN, *Seven Gothic Tales*

ONE

Each time he raised his eyes from the paper work, and even more each time he leaned his head against the top of the high, unyielding chair-back, he saw every detail, every outline in all its clarity, as though his gaze had newly acquired a subtlety and a sharpness, or as though the print were being reborn before his eyes with the same meticulous precision with which, in the year 1513, Albrecht Dürer had first engraved it. He had purchased it many years previously at an auction sale: one of those sudden, rash cravings for possession which, at certain times, in the presence of a painting, an etching or a book, took hold of him. He had competed for it with others who had themselves set their hearts on it, reaching a state of near hatred for the most tenacious of his rivals, who then casually abandoned it to him. The price corresponded to two months' salary, and when he came to handing over the money, the sum involved took him aback. At the time it was sizeable, and not only in relation to his ability to pay, but now, with the soaring rise of inflation and the tenfold increase in the value of the works of Dürer and all the other great engravers, it seemed derisory. He had taken it with him from one workplace to another, from one office to another, always choosing to hang it on the wall facing his desk, but of all those who, over the years, had passed through his office, only one (a talented swindler, who genially accepted the destiny which would see him taken from that office to become guest of some inhospitable prison for a period of years) had taken the time to look at it and appreciate it: to appreciate it fully, in the light of the most up-to-date catalogues of the print dealers of Paris and Zurich.

This appreciation had alarmed him somewhat; in an initial impulse of meanness or avarice he had decided to take it home, but the decision was forgotten almost as soon as it was made. He had long grown accustomed to having it there before him, in the many hours he spent in his office. *The Knight, Death and the Devil.* On the back, on the protecting cover, there were the titles, written in pencil in German and French: *Ritter, Tod und Teufel; Le Chevalier, la Mort et le Diable.* And mysteriously: *Christ? Savonarole?* Had the collector or dealer who had wondered about those two names perhaps thought that Dürer had wished to symbolize one or the other in the figure of the Knight?

Time and again, gazing at the print, he had asked himself that question. But now, leaning back in the chair in exhaustion and pain, he stared at it, groping for some meaning in that purchase made all those years ago. Death; and that castle in the background, unattainable.

With the many cigarettes he had smoked during the night, the ever-present pain had lost its heaviness and density, changing shade to a more diffuse agony. It was undoubtedly possible to give the names of colours to the different qualities and shifts of pain. At the moment it had changed from violet to red: flame red, in probing tongues which quite unpredictably pierced every part of his body, to linger there or fade away.

Automatically, he lit another cigarette, but would have let it burn out in the ashtray had not the Chief, on entering, launched into his customary tirade against the destructive habit of heavy smoking. A senseless vice, a death vice. He, the Chief, had given up smoking within the last six months, and was extremely proud of himself, but he still experienced, together with a certain pain, pangs of envy and rancour when he saw others smoke; both were nourished by the fact that, at the very time when the memory of smoking was to him like a paradise lost, the smell of smoke occasioned a discomfort which came close to nausea.

"Don't you feel suffocated in here?" said the Chief.

The Deputy picked up the cigarette from the ashtray and inhaled slowly and voluptuously. It was perfectly true. The atmosphere was suffocating. The room was full of smoke which hung thickly around the still burning lights; like a transparent curtain, it veiled the glass of the windows through which, flickeringly, morning was beginning to shine. He inhaled once more.

"I can understand," said the Chief in a tone of superior tolerance, "that certain people may lack the will power to kick the habit entirely, but to pursue a death of this kind with such stubbornness and self-indulgence ... My brother-in-law ..." He employed his brother-in-law, a chain-smoker deceased a few months previously, as a blind, in a delicate effort to avoid having to refer directly to the illness of which, plainly, the Deputy was intent on dying.

"I know. We were friends ... You, I imagine, will have already chosen your own style of death. I must get you to talk to me about it one of these days. Who knows, you might even persuade me to choose it too."

"I haven't chosen it, and it is not a thing that can be chosen; but now that I have given up smoking, I hope to die a different death."

"You are no doubt aware it was the converted Jews who invented the Catholic Inquisition in Spain."

He was not aware. And so: "I have never had much time for the Jews, strictly between you and me."

"I know, but I would have expected you to have some interest in converts." They were almost colleagues, having known each other for years, and so could indulge, but always without malice, in the occasional ironic, pointed or even sarcastic remark. The Chief let them pass on account of the unease occasioned by the incomprehensible loyalty of the Deputy towards him. Never had he met a Deputy of such loyalty; initially he had left no stone unturned in his efforts to locate a hidden reason; now he knew there was none.

"Converts or not, I've no time for them. You, on the other hand ..."

"I, on the other hand have no time for converts, Jewish or not: every convert opts for something worse, even when it seems better. The worst, in someone who is capable of conversion, always becomes the very worst of the worst."

"Conversion to not smoking has nothing to do with it: granted that conversion is generally an abomination."

"It has everything to do with it: because the tendency is to become persecutors of those who still smoke."

"How can you say that? Persecutors! If I were a persecutor, these offices would be filled with huge notices screaming No Smoking at you: it might be an idea – in spite of you, and for your own good. Because I am saying this for your good: my brother-in law ..."

"I know."

"So, let's say no more about it. As regards your philosophy on converts, I could produce arguments to annihilate you, just like that." The snap of the thumb and index fingers indicated the lightning speed of the act of annihilation. It was a gesture he employed frequently, because there was no limit to the number of things he planned to annihilate; and the Deputy, who sometimes attempted to imitate it, but without ever managing to produce the slightest snap, was prone to a childish envy on this account. "However, we have work to do. Come with me."

"Where?"

"You know already. Let's go."

"Isn't it a bit early?"

"No, it's already seven o'clock: I was deliberately killing time with your philosophy."

"Early, always early." He hated the police custom of executing warrants, carrying out house searches, routine investigations and door-to-door enquiries in the early hours of the morning or, more often than not, at the dead of night. Both fellow officers and the lower ranks considered it a pleasure to be savoured whenever the slightest opportunity or the remotest justification presented itself. The thunderous knock at the door behind which unwitting families were enjoying their rest, their sleep; at the very hour when sleep, once the weight of exhaustion has been lightened, becomes less dark, more open to dreams, more blissful; the terrified – Who's there? and the solemn, booming reply – Police; the door held barely ajar, the eyes, distrustful and sleep-filled, peering out; the violent shove at the door, the rush of bodies; and inside, the agitated awakening of the whole family, the voices of fear and bewilderment, the crying of the children ... For such a delight, there was not a man in the force, whatever his rank, who would think twice about his own lost sleep. The Deputy, however, loved to sleep, after at least an hour with a book, right through from midnight to seven o'clock, and on the rare occasions when – invariably because of the division to which he was attached – he had to take part in such operations, he was always tormented by a personal sense of anguished shame.

"It's seven o'clock," said the Chief, "and it takes at least half an hour to get to Villaserena. After all, in the circumstances, I can hardly allow myself any special consideration, not even for him."

"We have already allowed ourselves just that," said the Deputy ironically. "If it had been anyone else, we would have been there three hours ago, and already had the house upside down."

"No doubt," said the Chief, stung to the point of cynicism.

The black car waited for them in the courtyard – a beautiful, harmoniously colonnaded, baroque courtyard. There was no need to tell the policeman at the wheel where they were making for: everyone in the building which, buzzing as busily as any beehive, was even then coming back to life, was fully aware. How many calls, wondered the Deputy, had already gone out from that building to alert the President of the visit he was about to receive? The President: there was not the slightest need to add "of United Industries", because in that city, anyone referring to "the President" without further qualification had only one person in mind; for any other President, not excluding the President of the Republic, some specification was essential.

They remained silent for the entire half hour of the drive, or race, in the traffic which grew more frantic by the minute. The Chief cast and considered, recast and reconsidered what he would say to the President: concern was written on his face like the toothache. The Deputy knew him well enough to be able to decipher every detail of that concern: almost word for word; with each and every erasion, correction and replacement that he judged suitable for the case. A palimpsest.

They arrived at the villa. The officer at the wheel (I have been overcome by a sudden inhibition about using the word *driver:* with a sense of regret at having used it on other occasions; but will it ever again be possible to say, as was common in my childhood, *chauffeur?*) got out and rang the bell at the gatehouse long and imperiously. The Chief's toothache gave him a visible, stabbing pain: not like that, for God's sake! There are ways and ways. But he said nothing, out of deference to custom.

The Chief gave only his own name to the doorman who came forward. Not to mention the word Police seemed to him the first act of consideration due to the President: but the doorman was sufficiently quick-witted and experienced to grasp that he should announce – two gentlemen from the police, even if, as a Southerner, the word "gentlemen" stuck in his craw; he made up for it with the contempt he put into the pronunciation. He came back without saying a word: he opened the gate and signed to them to proceed along the avenue towards the villa which could be seen at the foot of the tree-lined driveway, in all its enchantment, in all its song. ("When a building sings, it is architecture.")

Everything – entrance hall, staircases, corridors, library and

President's studio – of a fragile, musical rococo, as though indeed a burst of song.

They had not long to wait: the President glided in silently from behind a curtain. He was clad in a velvet dressing-gown, but was already shaved and on the point of dressing with that severe and sure elegance which the fashion journals – now of each and every fashion – attributed to him. There hovered in the air around him an irritation at being compelled to delay his customary, almost lengendarily punctual, morning departure for the offices of United Industries, from whose top floor, as though in confidential familiarity with heaven, he took the daily, invariably correct, decisions which kept the whole country on the road to affluence and well-being; even if it was besieged on one side by the spectre of poverty, and on the other by that of plague.

"To what do I owe the pleasure of this unaccustomed visit?" asked the President, taking his time over shaking the Chief's hand and almost ignoring the Deputy's. He uttered the word "unaccustomed" as though watching it materialise in large italics.

The Chief spluttered, as everything he had prepared fled from his mind, like hydrogen from a punctured balloon. He said: "You knew Sandoz, the lawyer, well and . . ."

"We are friends," replied the President, "but as to knowing him well . . . you don't even know your own children well . . . in fact, you invariably know them badly, very badly indeed. In other words, Signor Sandoz is a friend of mine, we see each other a lot, we have interests which are, if not exactly in common, at least closely related. But you said, I think, *knew*: so . . ."

The Chief and the Deputy exchanged understanding glances. There flitted into those minds trained in distrust and suspicion, trained in the setting of word traps or in picking up stray words which could be converted into traps, the certainty that the President already knew – and it hardly came as a surprise, since there was no shortage of his acolytes in their offices – of the death of Sandoz. The Chief immediately put the thought aside, in the belief that for his part the President had a mind trained in not compromising his informers. He said: "Unfortunately, Signor Sandoz is no more: he was murdered this evening, probably some time after midnight."

"Murdered?"

"Murdered."

"Unbelievable! I left him just shortly before midnight. We said goodbye at the door of the La Vecchia Cucina restaurant ... Murdered! But why? And by whom?"

"If we knew, we would not be here taking up your time."

"Unbelievable!" repeated the President, but then he corrected himself. "Unbelievable! ... what am I saying? Nowadays in this country everything is believable, everything is possible ... I myself ..." He was unable to make up his mind, thought the Deputy, between pretending he wanted to show them out and admitting that he understood there was more to come and that he had other questions to answer. By placing his hands on the arms of the chair as though to raise himself and see them to the door, he chose the pretence; ill-advisedly because the Chief sensed it instinctively and, quite unconsciously, freed himself of the unease to which he had been prey until that moment. As was normal when beginning an interrogation, he settled into the armchair as though taking up residence in it. His voice trembled with the customary – *Say what you please, but I won't believe a word of it.* The well-prepared attack was launched – "We had to come and disturb you, at this inopportune hour, to ask you something that might be entirely meaningless, but could just as easily provide the starting point for our investigations: investigations which, I need hardly say, will not affect you, your person ..." He went on: "In one pocket of Sandoz's jacket, we found this card." He pulled out of his own pocket a little rectangular, ivory-coloured card. "On one side, typewritten, there is your name: CESARE AURISPA, PRESIDENT U.I. ... and on the other, in handwriting, *I'll kill you* ... a place-marker, as can be easily seen ... but the *I'll kill you*?

"A threat carried out there and then, you must have concluded. And, plainly, by myself in person." The President laughed: an ironic, indulgent, bitter laugh.

The professional reserve of the Chief vanished immediately. He protested with vehemence: "Whatever makes you say such a thing? For goodness sake ... I'd never forgive myself for thinking ..."

"Not at all," said the President generously, "you can forgive yourself. It's just that you've got it wrong: and we have seen too many men in your position fall in love with their mistakes, cultivate them like flowers, wear one or two in their lapel. It's normal, quite normal. That's how, some times, the most simple things in the world become damnably complicated ... your deductions were totally correct. That card marked my place at the dinner yesterday evening organised by the local cultural society named after Count de Borch; and it was me who wrote that *I'll kill you*. A little joke between me and Sandoz, as I'll explain. I gave the card to a waiter to take over to poor Sandoz, who was seated on the other side of the table, five or six places along from me ... The joke was that we were both pretending to be flirting with Signora De Matis, and since the lady, as had happened at other dinners of the same kind, had been seated beside him ... ?"

"You were pretending to be flirting, you say." The Chief adopted a tone of disbelief, an incautious trick of the trade. The President, in fact, noticed it; and with a touch of disgust:

"You can take my word for it; in any case, just look at her ..."

"I wouldn't dare doubt it," said the Chief. But the deputy thought to himself – you did doubt it, you are still doubting it: it's a credit to your profession, to our profession. In spite of his resolution not to speak, he directed a question at the President in the standard police form of a statement or assertion: "And Signor Sandoz replied by writing on the place marker in front of him ... ?"

The Chief looked over disapprovingly: as did the President, who seemed to become aware of his presence only at that instant. "Yes, he scribbled a reply. He was playing the game ... he said he accepted the risk, or something of that sort ..."

"But you haven't kept the card."

"I left it on the table. I might have stuck it back in the little ironwork stand; it was flower-shaped, if I remember correctly."

"Whereas the unfortunate Signor Sandoz put the one you sent to him in his pocket: absent-mindedly, automatically," said the Chief: scarcely concealing in the servility of the phrase a touch of incredulity, of suspicion.

"Exactly: absent-mindedly, automatically," approved the President.

"What a problem," said the Chief.

"Did you come here in the belief that I was the solution?" asked the President: ironic, annoyed, almost enraged.

"No, no, absolutely not. We came because it was necessary to clear up this detail, to get it out of the way at once; so as to be able to pursue other lines of enquiry."

"Do you have any other lines of enquiry?"

"For the moment, none at all."

"For what it is worth, and personally I believe it to be worth very little, I may be able to give you one." He remained silent for some time, leaving the Chief in a state of anxiety which to the Deputy appeared too clearly expressed to be true: just as the president's face also turned too excessively expressive: with the promise of what he was about to reveal and, simultaneously, with regret for the puny content of the revelation itself. And indeed: "It is not that it seems to me a line of enquiry with any real foundation; in fact it seems to me more of a joke: poor Sandoz too spoke of it as a joke ..." (Another joke, thought the Deputy, these people spend their lives making jokes.) "No later than yesterday evening, as we were making our way out of the restaurant, he told me he had received a threatening telephone call – perhaps one, perhaps

more than one, I can't recall – from a ... let me try to
remember from whom, because it couldn't be ... the words
coming into my head right this moment are ... the *Boys of
Ninety-nine* ... That can't be right: the *Boys of Ninety-nine*
were the ones who were called up after Caporetto in 1917:
'the Piave was murmuring', and all that ... Anyone of those
boys still alive would be nearly ninety today: and in any case,
it would be a reference to an indecently patriotic event ...
No, no, it couldn't be ... Let me think ..." They let him
think, until they saw his face light up with the relocated
memory. "That's it: *the Boys of Eighty-nine*, I think ... yes,
eighty-nine ... But not the boys, now that I think of it: the
children, perhaps ..."

"The Children of Eighty-nine," the Chief savoured the
words, but found there the bitterness of incomprehension.
"Eighty-nine, then. The children of the present year – 1989."

The Deputy, who, observing the outcome of the President's
efforts of memory, had thought that it would have
been much easier to remember the year Eighty-nine, since
only a very few days had passed since the New Year festivities,
than the year Ninety-nine for all its associations with the
Piave, found himself saying: "1789, more likely. A wonderful
idea, that."

Neither the President nor the Chief found this intrusion to
their liking. "You are always obsessed with history," said the
Chief. And the President said, "What idea?"

"That notion of Eighty-nine. Where else does the idea of
revolution spring from if not from that year? It does not
take much now to admit that, as they used to say of a certain
drink – it was the first and remains the best ... yes, quite
wonderful."

"Wonderful is hardly the word I would use." The President
gestured as though swatting a troublesome fly.

"Anyway, 1989 or 1789," said the Chief, "we will discover
which in due course. Indeed I am confident we will know
very soon ... What matters here and now, so as not to waste

your time, which I know is valuable, is this; we must know exactly what poor Signor Sandoz confided to you yesterday evening about these Children of Eighty-nine and their threats."

"For goodness sake, who said anything about confidences? He spoke to me with an offhand nonchalance. He was quite blasé about it. As I said, he was convinced it was a joke."

"But it was nothing of the kind," said the Chief: with a fondness for the Children of Eighty-nine which, for all its suddenness, gave every promise of developing bull-dog tenacity.

"I have nothing more to add," said the President, rising to his feet. "Try talking to other friends of poor Sandoz, or to his closest colleagues."

TWO

"So," said the Deputy, "exit the President."

"You'd prefer to hold him onstage?"

"Not exactly; it's just that I have a certain curiosity."

"Keep it to yourself," said the Chief: with irritation, brooking no opposition. As if to stress the point, he went on: "I know them, these curiosities of yours: they are so fine as to be practically invisible to the naked eye."

"Another reason for satisfying them."

"Quite the reverse! I can't see them, and neither can any man of down to earth, common sense; but the people who are the object of these attentions, sooner or later they become aware of them. And then the troubles start, with a vengeance. For the curious."

"I understand you," said the Deputy. He was rambling somewhat. Since the pain had long since succeeded in taking a grip, giving him colours, images, and above all thoughts (but not in the night-time hours, during which it seemed to have no bounds but to penetrate every part of the mind and of the universe), he now felt and saw it as a slow wave in its ebb and flow; grey, leaden. But the conversation with the President, arousing him to a state of suspicious attention, had been a diversion which he was now prolonging in the conversation with the Chief. So as a blandishment to him: "I am sure that you too must feel some measure of curiosity."

"Let's make an exception for once: tell me about your curiosity, which you seem to think I share."

"To know exactly what was written on the card Sandoz sent to Aurispa."

"Yes, I just may be curious: but on a personal, whimsical level that has nothing at all to do with the investigation we are embarking on."

"Are you curious or not?"

"I confess I am: but any investigation in this direction would hardly be viewed in a kindly light by the President."

"He was so vague, so offhand concerning Sandoz' reply which, call it a joke if you like, was still the last thing written by a man who was murdered immediately afterwards ... I would say it was our duty to make enquiries: as a pure formality, nothing out of the ordinary. To tie up this business, in other words."

"All right, I will drop you in front of the restaurant, and I'll send along two men to assist you in your search. But let's be clear about one thing: that card has no bearing on our enquiries."

"You've got a line of enquiry already?"

"I will have: within an hour or two."

"Dear God!" invoked the Deputy.

The Chief read the turmoil in his face: but restricted himself to a rancorous silence. Then, once they had arrived at La Nuova Cucina and the Deputy was on the point of getting out, he asked; "What exactly fails to convince you?"

"The Children of Eighty-nine. If you let the word out, you know what is going to happen: all the way from Sicily to the Swiss border, they'll turn up in their dozens."

"I won't say a word about them, if the friends and acquaintances of the victim do not oblige me with some confirmation, and with a few extra details thrown in."

"I have no doubt that you'll receive your confirmation and extra details."

"I have never seen you so optimistic."

"On the contrary, I have never been so pessimistic."

"I beg you," were the words, but spoken in tones of authority, "please do not make my poor head spin."

The Deputy made a gesture of compliance and obedience.

He went off to the café next door to phone the owner of the restaurant to get him to come and open up. While waiting, he had a drink.

The morning was glass clear and icy cold; as cold as the stinging pain in the joints of his bones. Nevertheless these eccentric, peripheral pains had the power to lessen the overwhelming central pain; or at least to give him that illusion.

He drank, one after the other, two cups of strong coffee. They said coffee deadened pain, but these coffees only gave him the lucidity to put up with it. His mind was, in the meantime, occupied with the refuse which would be in short time displayed before him. Garbage science. A parable, a metaphor: we are now concerned with garbage; searching for it, shaping it, reading it, seeking in it some trace of truth. In refuse. A journalist had once sought the secret of political secrets in the refuse of Henry Kissinger, and the American police the secrets of the Sicilian-American mafia in the refuse of Joseph Bonanno. "Garbage never lies," was now an accepted precept of sociology. But Bonanno's garbage had lied to police officer Ehmann: *Call Titone work and pay scannatore*. Nothing could be clearer, for Ehmann; if scannare in Italian means to *slaughter*, a scannatore is one whose job is to slaughter. It would have helped if he had known of *L'Aria del Continente*, the play by Nino Martoglio based on an idea from Pirandello, since it would have made him aware of the extent of the inferiority complex a Sicilian feels about his own dialect once he acquires a smattering of Italian. For this reason the Sicilian word Scanaturi had been, in the Bonanno household, Italianized to Scannatore. The jotting was no more than a note, an aide-memoire to remind the writer to pay a Sicilian-American joiner, Titone by name, for one of those huge, meticulously planed tables of strong wood on which the women – once in Sicily, now in America – knead the bread, make lasagne, tagliatelle, pizza or foccaccia. Scanaturi: "an instrument for kneading dough", in the definition given, in the year 1754, by the Jesuit Michele del Bono. Had Bonanno naively Italianized the word, or had he set out to play a joke for his own benefit, on Ehmann?

Odd, thought the Deputy, that the word joke should have made its appearance with such frequency in these last hours. And it was a joke that he was playing on his Chief. He was certain that Sandoz' card would not be found among the refuse of the night before. And in fact, after two hours and more of searching, it was not found. *Garbage never lies:* in this case by absence. It was a different thought that unnerved him: that mankind was heading for death in a sea of garbage.

THREE

So as not to give the Chief headaches, he listened in silence to the interrogation of the friends and colleagues of poor Sandoz (whom, when alive, no one would have considered calling poor, rich as he was in talent, possessions, power and women; and there was every good reason for doubting whether he had in fact been assumed, a few hours earlier, into the heaven of the poor). Some confirmed the broad outlines, others added new details. Yes, poor Sandoz had spoken of phone calls from the Children of Eighty-nine; but as a joke, since, among other things, the last caller had seemed to him to have a child's voice – thin, hesitant, almost babbling. And he had spoken reflectively of the other calls, four or five in all, which, as he recalled, had seemed to him made by different voices, belonging to people of varying ages. All disguised, obviously; so perhaps it had always been the same person on the telephone, making the first call with an old man's voice and, regressing, the last with the voice of a child. "The next time," Sandoz had told his secretary, "I'll get a call from a toddler." He joked about it; he had even told the secretary that he had his suspicions about who was playing jokes of this kind on him. The Children of Eighty-nine: what an odd notion! And everyone, including Sandoz, had thought of 1989; new-born revolutionaries, which explained the falling age of the callers.

"As you can see," said the Chief, "your 1789 has gone for a burton."

"Perhaps," said the Deputy.

"Far be it from me to deny that your pig-headedness has shown itself, occasionally, of some value. But right now, trust me, it would be better to pack it away for better days."

"I don't believe there will be a better time than this. But I have no wish to cause you headaches, or to upset you."

"Go on, upset me."

"All right. I believe that the joke – let's go on calling it a joke – was deliberately calculated to give rise to two successive hypotheses: the first, while Sandoz was still alive, and principally aimed at Sandoz himself, was that we were genuinely dealing with a joke – something innocuous and laughable; the second, once Sandoz had been murdered, that we were dealing with no such thing. For the first hypothesis, 1989, the comedy of people transforming themselves into the babes of some unspecified revolution, worked perfectly. What was it but a word, a mere word? For the second hypothesis, it is the threat, which begins to take concrete form with the murder of Sandoz, of imitating and rounding off the revolution of 1789, of renewing all its pomp and terrors, which works."

"I am in agreement that the two jokes, as you prefer calling them, are linked."

"Yes but there is another point on which we are not, and will not be, in agreement: that without our being aware of it, in the midst of the celebrations of the 1789 revolution, there was born a terrorist organisation utterly convinced of those principles, and now ready and dedicated to breaking the law to restore the part of that revolution which was once defeated; because this has to be the sense of the title Children of Eighty-nine. This association does not exist, but somebody wants to will it into existence, as a shield and a spectre for quite different purposes."

"And who, in your view, had this wonderful idea? Wonderful was your word, right from the first; love at first sight, a *coup de foudre*," said the Chief, with near hysterical irony.

"As to who had the idea, I do not know, and I do not believe we will ever know. But to judge from the effect it will in all probability produce, it is undoubtedly wonderful. Just think: now that the red flag no longer flies high, what revolutionary banner could be unfurled to seduce feeble minds, to attract the bored and the violent who need to dignify their instincts, or to appeal to those with a vocation for sacrifice and lost causes? I could add that your conviction that the children of Eighty-nine exist in the form they claim to proves just how brilliant the original idea was."

The Chief turned serious, solemn and peremptorily decisive: "Listen here; I let you have your way over the rubbish at the restaurant. A waste of time, both yours and of the two men, and God knows how much I could have done with them here ..." He sighed his habitual, long-suffering sigh over the shortage of men and equipment.

"I would not call it wasted time: the card, as I foretold, was not there."

"All the worse; we wasted time in the full knowledge that it would be wasted ... Now listen to me: I am no fool; I can see your suspicions and intentions quite clearly, and I know what you are driving at and where you want to bring me. And I am telling you quite bluntly – No. And not only because I have no inclination for suicide, but because the line you are following is lifted straight from fiction, from one of those books they call a classical detective novel, where the sharp-witted reader can guess, after the first twenty pages, how it is all going to turn out ... Let's forget about the novels, shall we? We'll proceed calmly, with deliberation, without any brainstorms, without impulsiveness, and above all without prejudice or preconceived ideas ... In any case, the whole affair is about to be handed over to a magistrate: if he turns out to have the same taste in novels as you, you can put your heads together and speculate to your hearts' content, and I'll wash my hands of the entire business ... Meanwhile, I would like to point out that in the course of your lucubrations, you have overlooked one hypothesis which seems to me promising: that someone present at the banquet may have noticed that little game with the cards and may have seen Sandoz slip the *I'll kill you* into his jacket pocket; and that he may just have decided to take advantage of it."

"A technically correct hypothesis, but, I believe, in the overall view of the matter, irrelevant."

"You never know. Check up. Make the cultural association hand over the list of the guests, and find out who, among the diners seated next to Sandoz and the President, had the opportunity to watch the game. And next, obviously, who among them had any motive for detesting Sandoz. And finally, no brainstorms; not a step without informing me first. All right?"

FOUR

Sandoz numbered an actor among his friends, and a colleague who remembered having seen them photographed together indicated him to the Chief as a possible perpetrator of the telephone joke. Since Sandoz had said he knew who was responsible for the joke, who could be more likely than someone with the professional ability? The actor had a certain reputation in the world of cinema and theatre, and the Chief recalled having heard him imitate a range of voices, from the guttural Catanian accents of Musco to the more polished, melodious tones of Ruggero Ruggeri. Without conviction, being now enamoured of the Children of Eighty-nine, he instituted a search the length and breadth of Italy for him. Finally they found him where they could have found him all the time, if they had taken the trouble to glance at the pages of the morning newspapers devoted to cinema and theatre.

Over the telephone, after listening to a cursory explanation of why he was being sought, the actor admitted that he had known Sandoz (a grudging admission, the only sort ever afforded to police questions), but not with sufficient intimacy to play jokes on him: and such a senseless joke into the bargain! Of itself, this served as the required corroboration for the police and the magistrature, who had taken over the conduct of the investigation, that there was a close connection between the phone calls from the Children of Eighty-nine and the murder. Meanwhile, as invariably occurred when responsibility for an investigation changed hands, the story about the Children of Eighty-nine leaked out. And obviously, since the year was 1989, almost all the newspapers assumed the name indicated a new-born, new style, different brand of terrorism. However, an anonymous phone call to the biggest circulation daily taxed the police, magistrates and journalists with ignorance and short sightedness, and pointed them in the direction of 1789. "We will re-establish the Reign of Terror," said the anonymous informant, adding that the execution of Sandoz – regrettably, not by guillotine – was only a foretaste of what lay ahead. A further call gave the group a more precise title: *Children of Eighty-nine, Saint-Just Action Group.*

"So you were right," said the Chief. What he paid in wounded pride, he believed he was repaid in generosity: the generosity of a superior who gives way to his deputy.

"Yes, but this is not the point. The point is that the Children of Eighty-nine are being born now: of mythomania, of boredom, maybe of a vocation for conspiracy and criminal activity, but they did not exist a moment before the radio, television and the newspapers carried stories about them. The calculation of the people who murdered Sandoz, or who had him murdered, has created them. They calculated that at the very least they would confuse us, and that at best some fool would answer the call and proclaim himself one of the Children of Eighty-nine."

"You've lost me. I cannot follow you in this work of fiction."

"I understand. Anyway, even if you did agree with me, we would still be out on our own."

A period of civic mourning and an official State funeral had been decreed for Sandoz, for who would now have had the audacity to lay to rest in a more humble tomb that victim of political criminality, of anti-democratic fanaticism and terrorist madness?

"I am glad to hear you acknowledge it: there would be no more than two of us, always assuming that your novel had the slightest element of credibility for me."

"Just to continue with the novel ... we are facing a problem, a dilemma: were the Children of Eighty-nine created murder Sandoz, or was Sandoz murdered to create the Children of Eighty-nine?"

"I'll leave it to you to solve that one. As far as I am concerned, and as far as this office is concerned, I proceed on the basis of established fact. Sandoz received menacing phone calls from the Children of Eighty-nine; Sandoz was murdered; the Children of Eighty-nine have claimed responsibility. Our job is to find them and bring them, as they say, to justice."

"The Children of Eighty-nine."

"The Children of Eighty-nine, precisely. And look; as regards that dilemma of yours, I could even, in an abstract way, as a game, as a purely literary concern, go along with the first of your two extremes: that the Children of Eighty-nine were born to dispatch Sandoz more conveniently and make our task in getting to the guilty party or parties more difficult, or even downright impossible. As to the second possibility, the one about Sandoz being murdered so as to give birth to the Children of Eighty-nine, I'll leave that one to you. And have fun with it."

"For over half a century, in all branches of the police, we have had to swallow so many toads that I believe we have earned the right to a little fun. Apart from the many I have personally swallowed in nearly thirty years with this division."

"One toad more, one toad the less ... What can I say? If you really see this business shaping up as yet another toad to swallow, get ready to swallow it."

FIVE

He was disobeying, being disobedient. In a little sitting-room in the De Matis house, with the lady herself at his side. She had sat down beside him, perhaps because curiosity had over-come her to the point that she instinctively imagined that physical proximity would create the best conditions for shared confidences.

"The moment the porter told me that a police officer wanted to speak to me, I understood: I have no doubt that you want to know about the cards that Sandoz and Aurispa exchanged three evenings ago."

She had an intelligent face, and beautiful eyes which seemed to flicker with an amused, ironic light. Anything but unat-tractive. Aurispa had said that a glance at her was enough to make anyone aware that the desire to have her at your side could never be more than a game, a fiction, but that remark only revealed that he had the decidedly unsubtle view of female beauty of a purchaser whose only ambition was not to be short changed. She was thin but not displeasingly so; she could be said to be slight, and her movements and gestures were light and almost fluttery.

"I have to say at the outset that I am indeed a police officer, but I came to you in a private capacity and in total secrecy."

"Tell me the truth, do you suspect him?"

"Do we suspect whom?"

"Him, Aurispa." The amused, ironic light seemed to have spread out, adding a splendour to the eyes of indefinable blue, of indefinable violet.

"No, he is not a suspect."

34

"It would give me enormous pleasure to know that at least the shadow of suspicion had fallen on him."

"Really?"

"Yes, enormous satisfaction. And I still hope it will happen: there are so many murky matters in which he has a hand."

"Why would it give you such satisfaction?"

"I could say to you: for the sake of justice, but it would not be the whole truth. Basically it is because I do not like him, I find him repulsive. He is such a cold man and he seems to exist only in profile, as though on a coin, on various coins."

"Anything in particular?"

"No, nothing ... or rather, something, but something so vague that you cannot put your finger on it. But then, I always allow myself to be guided by vague, indefinite impressions, and I am never wrong, believe me ... but I see you won't be giving anything away. So let's see how good I am at making out what's behind your questions."

Intelligent, very intelligent, thought the Deputy, and the reflection gave him a feeling of near panic. To gain time, to purify the questions of the suspicions which Signora De Matis was prepared to detect in them, he said: "They are not really questions, the things I want to put to you."

"Out with them, then," said Signora De Matis, even more amused.

"I am engaged on an unremarkable, straightforward reconstruction of the last hours of Signor Sandoz. It is the sort of thing we are obliged to do even in those cases, like the present one, when we are convinced beforehand that it serves no useful purpose."

"Unremarkable, straightforward ... serving no useful purpose." The Signora's voice echoed his. She played her part in the game with ironic comprehension and indulgence, but also with barely restrained laughter. "So what is the question?"

"As I said, it is hardly a question at all ... I take it you are aware that the two of them were engaged in a ... shall we say romantic game, at your expense. Aurispa regretted not having you at his side and pretended he was in the grips of uncontrollable jealousy because Sandoz twice in as many days had had the good fortune of a place beside you."

"It had occurred more than twice. I could never understand why at those infernal official or society dinners they nearly always put me alongside that Sandoz – he used to bore me to death. Not only that, that little game of theirs, which you call romantic, bored me to distraction, or rather enraged me. It was as if they said to each other: Poor thing, she's so old, so unattractive that we really should give her at least this satisfaction. I do not need anyone to tell me that I am not pretty, and I am well aware that I am getting on in life, but that does not seem to me a sufficient reason why those two brainless creatures should dedicate a whole evening to letting me know it."

"No, not at all, you mustn't think that," said the Deputy, conscious of his own hypocrisy, because he had learned from Aurispa that things stood exactly as she had understood.

"Please, don't you start romantic games with me."

"It is not a romantic game. You ... forgive me, it is the first time I have met you and I do not imagine we will have the opportunity to meet again; you are so radiant ..." The word came to him unbidden, as though he had fallen in love on the instant. The pain pressed in on him more and more sharply, as though to make him aware of the other, the only love now available to him.

"Radiant. Very gracious of you. I will remember that. There are not many joyful things left to one at this point in life. You know I am almost fifty ... but let's get back to the question, shall we?"

"Yes, the President sent the card over to Sandoz; written on it were the words ..."

"I'll kill you."

"Did Sandoz write his reply on the same card?"

"No, he stuck Aurispa's card in his pocket, after giving it to me to read, with the delight, so it seemed to me, of a autograph hunter who has finally managed to secure a much desired specimen. He scribbled out his answer on his own place-marker, which was there in front of him, clasped onto a kind of iris which was too silvery to be genuine silver."

"And what did he write on his card?"

"The odd thing was that he did not let me read it, and I had not sufficient curiosity to peer over his shoulder while he was writing. He simply bored me, as did that stupid game of theirs ..."

"Do you remember who Aurispa was sitting beside? I imagine he would have been seated between two women."

"Yes, between two women: Signora Zorni and Signora Siragusa. But since Signora Zorni was seated on his right – you know who I mean; pretty enough, even if, to my mind, a bit empty-headed, but with just the right degree of empty-headedness to transform a pretty woman into a ravishingly beautiful one in the eyes of most men – he lavished more attention on her than on the other."

"You saw the card arrive at its destination?"

"Not exactly: I watched Sandoz look over at Aurispa with great attention, with a sense of anxiety ... I had the impression he was studying the impact with much more interest than their futile little game warranted ... then I saw him smile. I turned to look at Aurispa, and he was smiling as well: but both wore a smile that was, how shall I put it? ... strained, sour ... That exchange of smiles between them made a deep impression on me: that's why, when Sandoz was murdered a few hours later, I asked if you in the police had suspicions regarding Aurispa."

"No, we don't have any."

"Then you should. Maybe it goes back to the first time I heard the word, and maybe it is just childish, but I still associate the police with the idea of polish ... you know what I mean ... cleanliness ... is there cleanliness in the police?"

"As far as there can be."

"And as far as can be, there ought to be suspicions

regarding Aurispa, but there is very little to be done, isn't that so?"

"Not a great deal."

"If you tell me there is not a great deal to be done, I think it can be deduced that there is nothing to be done. The thing is that you appear to suffer over that."

"I suffer over so many things now."

"I would really love to know why you joined the police."

"From time to time I ask myself the same question, but I have never managed to give myself a precise answer. Sometimes I unearth a dignified, high-minded reply, that soars upwards like a tenor's chest notes: more frequently the replies are more humdrum ... the necessities of life, chance, laziness ..."

"You are Sicilian, aren't you?"

"Yes, but from the cold side of Sicily: from a tiny village in the interior, among the mountains, where the snow lies for long periods in the winter. A Sicily which never figures in anyone's imagination. I have never again in all my life felt such intense cold as I did in that village."

"I remember that cold Sicily as well. Usually we went in summer, but some times there were additional trips at Christmas. My mother was Sicilian, and her parents never left that village; they never ever moved from that great house of theirs which was cool in summer but bitterly cold in the winter months. They died there and my mother died there too, before them. I never went back. I receive a letter after every All Souls' day from one of my relatives telling me about his visit to the graves, about the flowers and candles he brings along to decorate them. It is almost a reproach to me, because, emotionally and sentimentally, the fact that my mother wanted to go back there to die ought to count for something. I am afraid the truth is that even this choice of my mother's, if I think about it, causes me some dismay. It is simply not possible to love a place or a people to that extent, especially when it was a place where you suffered so much, and a people with whom you do not have anything at all in common. My mother experienced only pain from her life there, and finally rebelled and fled, and yet she felt a love for it which went beyond the tomb ... And do you want to know why the thought of that gives me such a sense of dismay? Because every so often I bewilder myself by feeling an echo of the same love, of the same memory, of the same choice ... but perhaps it is only an expression of that remorse my relative is so anxious to make me feel."

"I don't know if you have read that page of D. H. Lawrence's on Verga's novel *Mastro Don Gesualdo*. At one point he says: but Gesualdo is Sicilian, and it is here that the difficulty arises."

"The difficulty ... Yes, perhaps that's where my difficulty in living comes from." As if to change subject, very deliberately: "You read a lot, don't you? I read very little, and now I find more enjoyment in re-reading: you discover things which were not there at the first reading ... I mean, were not there for me ... Do you know what I am re-reading? *Dead Souls*: packed full of things which were not there before; and who can tell how many other things I would find if I were to return to it twenty years from now? Enough of books. We were talking about the reasons which impelled you to join the police."

"Perhaps, since crime belongs to us, to get to know it a little better."

"Yes, it's true: crime does belong to us: but there are some people who belong to crime."

SIX

Signora Zorni. Unquestionably beautiful, to the point of bland perfection; with a garulousness to match that perfection; head in the clouds, abstracted, afloat in the most celestial and unattainable heavens of a stupidity which she knows is both celestial and unfathomable; as do the genuinely intelligent, but they, experiencing that stupidity as a seductive force, fear it. She never seemed quite to grasp any question put to her, but the overall sense of the enquiry must, in some fashion, have nested in some recess of her beautiful head, since a reply could eventually be put together, even if it entailed picking and choosing the pieces which fitted best from a pile of multi-coloured stones, like a mosaicist. An operation the Deputy carried out as he went along, and we will follow suit; if it is to the detriment of the portrait, it is perhaps to the betterment of the narrative.

Yes, she knew about the half-pitying, half-mocking game which the two of them played on Signora De Matis: the President had informed her. She had seen the President write the *I'll kill you*, and had laughed at the idea, even if, she was anxious to add, she did not herself consider Signora De Matis as plain as many people thought: on the contrary, she was quite handsome, in her own way. And she had read Sandoz's answering card.

"Do you remember it?"

"Of course I do; I am blessed with a good memory as well." That "as well" spoke volumes for her confidence in her looks. "It was two lines of verse."

"Verse?"

"Yes, there were two short sentences written as lines of poetry; they even rhymed. They seemed to come from a song, and I had a terrible urge to hum them." She began humming them for him, using the tune from a melancholic number in vogue several years earlier. "I have no doubt that you will try: But who'll be victor, you or I?"

The Deputy felt a sense of exultation, but only said: "The President read the card aloud, or gave it to you to read . . ."

"No, he didn't give it to me; I read it while he was reading it himself. Then he slipped it into his pocket."

"Are you quite certain about that – that the President put it in his pocket?"

"Absolutely so." At that moment, a look of concern appeared on her face. "Does he insist that he didn't?"

"Even if that were so, would you continue to be sure that he did?" His words were intended purely to cause her a moment of anxiety, to upset that icy perfection, reminiscent of a newly excavated, totally intact statue.

"He is a gentleman of such irreproachable ways that I would begin to entertain the tiniest doubt."

"You can continue to be certain: the President claimed that he put the thing in his pocket mechanically; only he then, equally mechanically, threw it away."

The Signora gave a sigh of relief, the carefully cultivated image re-absorbing that moment of life. The Deputy thought that she did not really deserve to be called stupid, considering that, according to current hazy opinion, it's not possible in Italy to brand anyone as stupid.

Leaving Signora Zorni's house, he felt numbed. Drawing precise replies from a speech that resembled the Trevi Fountain – cascades, sprays, streams and torrents of running water – induced in him a feeling of tension, followed by weariness and numbness. His pain too was numb, less sharp but more dull and diffuse. Strange how physical pain, even when its source is stable and, unless deteriorating, unalterable, can still grow, diminish, change in intensity and quality according to opportunities and encounters.

He walked under the colonnades in the piazza, his mind occupied with that card, with those lines from the song; with Signora Zorni, young and lovely, with a body of lithe harmony: but how much more beautiful and desirable – in those flashes of desire which momentarily pierced his pain – was Signora De Matis, for all her fifty years.

He relished the colonnades, and enjoyed strolling at ease among them. In the island which had given him birth, there was no city which boasted colonnades such as these. Arches make the heavens more lovely, in the words of the poet. Do colonnades make cities more civil? It was not that he did not love the land where he was born, but all those invariably bitter and tragic events which day after day made the news there caused him a sort of resentment. Not having been back for years, he searched for it, behind mere occurrences, in his memory, in the emotion of something which no longer existed. An illusion, a mystification; as an emigrant, an exile.

SEVEN

There could be no half-measures with his disobedience. He had taken a chance with Signora Zorni, and the results would be apparent in due course. While neglecting to recommend silence to her – a recommendation which everyone, everywhere is irresistibly driven to break – he had none the less done everything in his power to convey the impression that his investigations were purely formal and superfluous, and a downright nuisance even for the people charged with carrying them out. It was, however, unthinkable that she had such a feeble memory as to totally forget, and, having not forgotten, that she would forgo the pleasure of informing one, two or more of her friends; and that from one woman to the next, the news would not reach the President's ears, and from the President the Chief's, or those of the occupant of a higher, much higher, position. Things stood differently with Signora De Matis: there was no such risk. Between the two of them, there had been the kindling of the spark of fondness, and a kind of complicity had been established.

From what he had heard about the exchange of cards, a question formulated itself in his mind, a question he had to put to a person able to provide a definite answer.

Kublai Travel Agency: proprietor, Dr Giovanni Rieti – doctor in what had never been satisfactorily established. An acquaintanceship of long standing, perhaps able to be considered a friendship, at least on account of the story of human tenderness which lay behind it. It had begun with their fathers in 1939: the Deputy's father, a local government officer in the Sicilian town where the father of Dr Rieti, a Jew, had happened to be born. Signor Rieti senior, in a state of despair, had come to the town from Rome, anxious to ascertain if in his birth certificate there might be some pretext for not considering him Jewish in the strict sense of the term. There being none, they – civil servants, mayor, Archpriest, municipal guards – made one up. Fascists to a man, each with party membership card in his pocket and badge in his lapel; if the Archpriest had neither card nor badge, he was Fascist in spirit. But all were unanimous that they could not abandon Signor Rieti, plus his wife and children, to the mercy of a law that was intent on his ruin. So they forged the documents in the duly accepted form, because to them the fact that a man was Jewish meant nothing if he were in danger, if he were in despair. (What a great country Italy was in these matters, and perhaps still is!)

They heard nothing more in his family of the Rieti family, and even if he retained some recollection of the case as one which had, among the many which had arisen in the first ten years of his life, made its mark, he had none the less forgotten the name. However one evening, in the city which had now been his home for some years, he attended a party in the prefect's office and there he was introduced to a Dr Rieti, who, on hearing his name, asked if he were Sicilian, if he were from such and such a town and if he had a relative who was in local government. It was like finding each other after years.

They met up on other occasions, with increasing frequency, until the Chief, with great tact and hinting at weighty matters left unsaid, advised him not to let himself be seen too often in the company of Dr Rieti. Still giving the impression of leaving the bulk of his information unspoken, he let it be understood that he had been tipped off by that service which in other times and in other countries would be called "intelligence"; which perhaps here and now did not merit the title intelligent; but, be that as it may, who were aware of certain things and who in any case – this was the gist of the Chief's talk – "knew each another", this being the very peak of the endeavours to which the Intelligence Services of every country dedicated themselves. Knowing each other, they knew Dr Rieti, and while it was permissible for them to be in communication with him, it was ill-advised for any other officer of the State, and especially so for a member of the police force.

The Deputy had continued to meet Dr Rieti, but with greater caution; he gave up meeting him for an aperitif in a bar, or for a meal in a restaurant, since suspicions regarding possible secret activities of his could arise if he spent his free time in the agency, if he were unusually well-informed on economic or financial deals, on internal rivalries inside the political parties, on the making and unmaking of alliances, on events in the bishop's palace or in terrorist circles.

On account of his illness, and of his work which took longer and became more of a burden as his illness grew more severe, he had not seen him for some two months. Dr Rieti greeted him with effusive cordiality, expressing his delight at seeing him in such excellent health. "I knew you were not well. Some one from your office told me a couple of evenings ago. But you look all right now. A bit slimmer, certainly, but they tell us nowadays that losing weight does nothing but good."

"You don't sound convinced."

"I admit it. When I see what my friends and relatives have to do to lose weight, and the troubles they put themselves through, it's my view that all these various dietologists and inventors of diets should receive the same treatment as drug pushers . . . what illness did you have, exactly?"

"To be exact, an illness for which I should be receiving cobalt therapy, or something of that sort."

"I had no idea it was anything so serious."

"It's even worse. I am dying," he said, with such serenity that the other felt the words he was about to speak freeze from sheer insincerity. He muttered only a "My God"

45

quietly, then after a long silence: "But a course of treatment ..."

"I have no desire to die fortified by the religious comforts of science, because not only are they as religious as the other sort but they are even more harrowing. If I were ever to feel the need of comfort, I would have recourse to the more ancient rites. In fact I would be quite glad to feel such a need, but I simply don't." He continued in an offhand tone, almost with delight: "Have you noticed? It is impossible to be bored in this country: we are all Children of Eighty-nine now."

"Indeed, Children of Eighty-nine." With irony, with malice.

"What do you make of it?"

"I think it is all so much hot air, pure fantasy. And you?"

"So do I."

"I am glad you agree. I read in the papers that your office is taking the whole thing seriously."

"Yes, of course, Do you expect them to miss out on such a splendid invention?"

"That's it exactly. It seems to me something invented round a coffee-table, as a game, as a calculation ... what is going to become of these poor devils, these poor idiots who want to continue believing in something after Krushchev, after Mao, after Fidel Castro and now with Gorbachev? They must be thrown some kind of sop, something which can be tossed back in the oven after two hundred years, something soft and scented with celebrations, rediscoveries and reassessments: and inside the same hard stone to break the teeth."

Always the same with Rieti: complete agreement over the evaluation of the facts, over their interpretation and the identification of their origin and purpose. Most frequently speaking of them hazily, by allusion, in parables or in metaphors. It was as if the same circuits, the same logical processes operated in both their minds. A computer of distrust, of suspicion, of pessimism. Jews, Sicilians: an atavistic affinity in their condition. Of energy. Of defence. Of suffering. A sixteenth-century Tuscan once wrote that the Sicilians are of a dry intelligence. So too are the Jews. But war had now descended on them: war by different means, but war none the less.

"I should like to ask you for the first time since we met –" and with these words he revealed his knowledge of the real, secret activity of Dr Rieti – "a precise question: what was the relationship between Sandoz and Aurispa?"

"They detested each other."

"Why?"

"I don't know what set them off on their mutual detestation, and it is not something which it would be easy to establish, because from what I hear they were school-friends. I do know that they each dedicated themselves with a will – all the while maintaining a relationship of seeming friendship – Aurispa to ruining Sandoz's business and Sandoz, with less success, to ruining Aurispa's. The consequence was that Sandoz, who had no intention of settling for second place, decided on a policy of blackmail, but here too with negligible results. Obtaining a warrant for Aurispa's arrest, maybe even one which ended after a few months in an acquittal for lack of proof, had become the dream of his life. It never became anything other than a dream."

"What were the grounds for blackmail?"

"I understand that the least ludicrous was based on a large scale act of corruption and fraud perpetrated by Aurispa against the State, for which Sandoz was in possession of proof, or believed he was. However I don't believe he would ever have gone to the length of making a statement to the police. There would have been reactions, counter-moves, and he would certainly not have emerged unscathed. Aurispa's only fear would be that Sandoz might have gone completely insane, because as long as he remained in possession of his faculties he would never have dared shake the columns, with the risk of bringing down the temple on his own head as well, their temple, the temple of so many Italians who matter . . .

The other grounds for blackmail were concerned with private matters, and they were at least thirty years out of date. Women, cocaine: what impression did he imagine they were going to make at this stage?"

"What about their business affairs?"

"War, war of every type. There is so much of it in the world ... and so much trade in arms, poisons."

"Do I understand you to be saying that you do not see the hand of Aurispa in the murder of Sandoz ... let me phrase that better ... you do not believe that the threats issued by Sandoz would have constituted sufficient reason for wanting him eliminated?"

"Exactly."

"Another reason, then."

"You used the correct term: sufficient. Sandoz's threats did not constitute sufficient reason for Aurispa to want him out of the way, but at a certain point, when other needs became more urgent, in the preparation of some project or other which, when subjected to cool examination, did not necessarily require the elimination of Sandoz, well ... the opportunity presented itself, as the proverb has it, of killing two birds with one stone."

"You mean that the victim could easily not have been Sandoz, but some one else with, what shall we say, equal qualifications? However, since Sandoz was more of a nuisance than any of the other candidates, the choice fell on him."

"Exactly."

"That is my opinion too. Immediately after listening to Aurispa, I said to my superior, who obviously takes no heed at all of my dilemma: the problem is whether the Children of Eighty-nine were created to kill Sandoz or whether Sandoz was killed to create the Children of Eighty-nine. And I tend to resolve my dilemma in the sense you indicate: that with one stone they have killed two birds: Primarily that of creating the Children of Eighty-nine ... but why?"

"As to why, I would say that through an ancient premonition, and a not so ancient admonition we know without knowing ... In our childhood we felt, rather than really knew, a power that today might be called total criminality, a power that, paradoxically, could be regarded as wholesome and healthy: always granted that it was crime, and comparing it to the schizophrenic criminality of today. The criminal nature of that power took the form principally of not permitting any other crime apart from the much vaunted, aesthetically embellished crime committed by itself ... there is no need for me to say that I prefer schizophrenia to good health, as I believe you do too. The important thing is that this schizophrenia has to be taken into account if certain otherwise inexplicable phenomena are to be explained. By the same token, it is vital to make allowances for the force of stupidity, of sheer stupidity insinuating itself and prevailing ... There is one power which can be seen, named and counted, but there is another which cannot be counted, which is without name or without names and which swims underwater. The visible power is in permanent conflict with the underwater power, especially at the moments when it has the gall to break surface with vigour, that is to say with violence and bloodshed: but the fact is that it needs to behave that way ... I trust you will not object to this piece of homespun philosophy, but where power is concerned, I have no other."

"There are grounds for suspecting, in other words, that there is in existence a secret constitution whose first article runs: The security of power is based on the insecurity of the citizens."

"Of all the citizens, in fact. Including those who, spreading in-security, believe themselves to be safe ... this is the stupidity I was referring to."

"Then we are tied up inside a *sotie* ... but let us get back to today's goings-on. Even if the newspapers have made no mention of it, you undoubtedly know all about the cards which Sandoz and Aurispa exchanged at that banquet as if it were a game ... what did you make of that?"

"It seemed to me a fact of some importance, but not one from which it would be possible at this moment to formulate reliable conclusions. A genuinely ambiguous fact, which could be clarified only by ascertaining the role of Aurispa in the whole business ... if he were the prime mover, if he were involved at the highest levels, he must have calculated that with that bit of nonsense over the cards he would, because of the way it occurred, have immediately been ruled out of the enquiries; if his part were secondary, it is also possible that he was not kept informed of the timing of the action; in that case it becomes feasible to believe in the chance nature of that game and in a fortuitous, and even fortunate, coincidence."

"I would go along with the hypothesis that he was involved at the highest levels."

"Perhaps, perhaps ..." said Rieti, but as though speaking out of courtesy. Plainly he knew something more, or believed he did. It was not right to press him on that point, so the Deputy said:

"One more question, perhaps the most indiscreet I can ask you: in your, let's say, functions, in the tasks you perform [the time for allusions was past; it was now the hour of truth for their acquaintanceship, or friendship, as for everything else] are you more interested in the business affairs pursued by Sandoz, until yesterday, or in those of Aurispa?"

"Of both, regrettably, although rather more, until yesterday, as you put it, in those of Sandoz;" with an expression in which the disgust for that business was possibly also disgust with himself.

EIGHT

He returned to find the whole police-station buzzing like a bee
hive gone berserk. One of the children of Eighty-nine had
been captured while making a phone-call. It turned out to be
one of those cases which exist to defy all laws of probability.
On the outskirts of the city, a deaf-mute was sitting on a park
bench, three or four metres from a public phone-box inside
which was a youth who, while talking, kept glancing nervously over his shoulder. For anyone other than a deaf-mute,
accustomed to picking up the silent shaping of words on lips,
the experience would have been like staring at a fish in an
aquarium. He read a dozen times on the lips of the youth
making the call the words – Children of Eighty-nine, Revolution, and Virtue. The deaf-mute happened to have in his hand
a newspaper carrying reports of the Children of Eighty-nine,
and in his pocket a marker pen with scarlet ink. He scrawled
on the paper – Children of Eighty-nine – and went off in
search of a policeman. He located a member of the local city
force who was equipped with a pistol suspended from his
waist, but who in every other way could hardly have been less
suited to the job. He grew faint on merely reading the writing: he pretended not to take the business seriously, to regard
it as a joke, to dispatch the deaf-mute with a little slap on the
cheek. When the other, with the aid of dramatic and excited
gestures, persevered, the policeman gave in and allowed himself to be escorted to the phone-box.

The youth was still inside and still talking: he was summar-
ising for the benefit of the switchboard operator of some
newspaper, duly trained in techniques of giving enough rope

to callers of that kind, a chapter of Mathiez's *French Revolution*, which he had only just read himself. Since, to the best of his recollection, the police had never managed to catch anyone phoning to claim responsibility for terrorist crimes or for kidnappings, irrespective of the length of the call, he felt, although nervous, safe. The policeman waited behind a magnolia bush until the call was over, crept up silently behind the youth, then leaned heavily on his back so as to leave him in no doubt about the pistol pressed against his kidneys. Fortunately for both their sakes he had forgotten to remove the safety-catch. In this condition, closely followed by the deaf-mute, he marched him to the nearest police station; this turned out to be not particularly near, so he was obliged to declare on several occasions to the crowd which began to form as he made his way – and which had become a triumphal procession long before they reached their destination – that the prisoner was an alleged member of the Children of Eighty-nine: never forgetting, as the law requires, the word "alleged", which is, as anyone familiar with current journalistic parlance will be aware, a synonym for established guilt. However, at a certain point, listening to the muttering of the crowd at his back, he found himself coming out in a cold sweat, fearing that their inclination was to implement swift justice rather than put up with the law's delays, with the risk that things might take an ugly turn for him, constrained as he would be to uphold the law's delays.

As God willed it, they arrived safely at a police station where all three – policeman, deaf-mute and child of Eighty-nine – were loaded into a van and dispatched to headquarters.

The youth was now in the Chief's office. Initially he had attempted to deny the content of the phone-call, but the deaf-mute was there at hand, implacably willing to write out the entire text, even if with occasional gaps. Finally, he caved in and made an admission, but insisted it had been a joke. That was not yet the whole truth, because he had believed that that call would have gained him admission to the Children of

Eighty-nine, or at least advanced his candidacy. Joke or demented act of self-assertion, a glance at him was enough to make clear that he could not have been in any way implicated in the murder of Sandoz. This thought ran through the Deputy's mind the moment the door of the Chief's office opened slightly. The boy was in a state of collapse while the chief radiated, like a halo round his massive head, the weary satisfaction of the athlete who has breasted the tape first.

He closed the door gingerly behind him, barring the frenzied, avid stares of the reporters congregated in the corridor. Among them, preening himself and foaming like a thoroughbred stabled among pit-ponies, stood the Great Journalist. With his articles, from which the moralists without morals drank their fill week in, week out, he had acquired a reputation for being relentless and implacable; a reputation which boosted his price among those who felt the need to buy silence and freedom from obtrusive attention.

As the Deputy made his way towards his office, the Great Journalist stopped him and requested an interview: "a brief one, very brief", he specified. The Deputy made a gesture more of resignation than of assent, while from the surrounding crowd murmurs of protest were raised.

"A private matter," said the Great Journalist, to the accompaniment of a chorus of ironic, incredulous remarks – "I bet", or "Sure", or "No doubt."

In the office, seated facing each other – a desk covered with papers, books and cigarette-packets between them – eyeing each other in wordless distrust as though locked in a conflict to determine who could remain silent longest, the Great Journalist reached into his pocket for pencil and notebook.

The deputy raised the index finger of his right hand and waved it in a slow but definitive No.

"An automatic gesture, a professional reflex ... I have only one question to ask, and I do not expect an answer."

"Then why bother?"

"Because neither you nor I are idiots."

"I am very grateful ... What is your question?"

"This story of the Children of Eighty-nine, was it you in the police force who invented it, or was it handed to you prepackaged?"

"I will give you your answer: it was not us who invented it."

"So they delivered it ready-made?"

"Could be ... that is my own suspicion, but it is no more than a suspicion."

"Does the Chief believe that too?"

"I don't think so, but you'd do better asking him."

The Great Journalist now wore a perplexed, mistrustful look. He said: "I did not expect you to reply, and instead you did: I expected you to brush aside my suspicions, and instead you added your own. What's going on?" His mind, as could be seen from his face, was a morass of discarded ideas, of corrections, of rethinking and of hesitancy. "So what is going on?" This time the words were tinged with anxiety.

"Nothing at all, I would say." Then, to insult him: "Have you ever heard of the love of the truth?"

"Vaguely." He spoke with disdainful irony, as though cynically noting the insult were the only means of reacting to it: he was looking down on an individual far beneath his notice.

The Deputy returned to the attack with an "Indeed, indeed", and added: "Tomorrow, then, I expect to read an article of yours setting out all the suspicions and doubts which I, in my personal capacity, have just confirmed."

The Great Journalist was red with rage: "You know perfectly well that I will never write it."

"Why should I know such a thing? I am still full of faith in humankind."

"We are in the same boat," His anger was tempered by a touch of frailty, of weariness.

"Don't you believe it. I have already landed on a desert island."

NINE

The conversation had left him drained, but the pain had gone: it cowered like a beast – squat, ferocious and repulsive – lying in ambush in one sole point of his body, of his being. The final words of the conversation, however, left him with a yearning for the deserted island, for a spot where, as though huddled over some map, he could give free rein to an ancient dream and an ancient memory: in as much as certain things from childhood and adolescence were now ancient to him. *Treasure Island*: a book, someone had said, which was the closest resemblance to happiness attainable. He thought: tonight I will re-read it. His memory of it was clear, since he had already re-read it many times in that old, unlovely edition they had once given him. In the course of his transfers from one city to the next, from one house to another, he had lost many books, but not this one. Aurora Publishers: yellowing paper, which after all these years seemed to have left the print parched and faded, and on the cover, from the black-and-white version of the film, a scene featuring a feckless and lacklustre Jim Hawkins together with Wallace Beery's unforgettable Long John Silver. The same man had been equally unforgettable as Pancho Villa, so much so that after having seen both films it was impossible to read either Stevenson's novel or Guzman's work on the Mexican Revolution without the characters presenting themselves with the physique, the gestures and the voice of Wallace Beery. He thought of all that the cinema had meant to his generation, and wondered if it would have a comparable impact on the new generation, and whether that scaled-down cinema, totally insufferable to him, given on television could ever have any impact at all.

He returned to the island, and a new character, Ben Gunn, appeared before him. His mind was so free, so unfettered and capricious, that from Ben Gunn, via a detail he suddenly recalled, he moved on to think about the advertising industry that threatened to flood the world. Even the producers of Parmesan cheese undoubtedly paid their toll to advertisers, but not a single advertising executive had ever remembered Doctor Livesey's snuff-box. He gleefully imagined the poster or full-page ad that could be made from that scene: Doctor Livesey proffering, to potential buyers, the open snuff-box with a piece of Parmesan inside, just as he did in the narrative to Ben Gunn, himself a great lover of cheese. "A delicious cheese, produced in Italy," the doctor would be saying, or something of the sort.

Meantime, his eyes were fixed on *The Knight, Death and the Devil*. Perhaps Ben Gunn, from Stevenson's description of him, had some resemblance to Dürer's Death. The thought prompted him to view Dürer's Death as in a grotesque light. The weary appearance of Death had always unsettled him, as if it implied that Death arrived on the scene wearily and slowly at the point when people were already tired of life. Death was weary, his horse was weary, both a far cry from the horses of the *Triumph of Death*, or *Guernica*. Death, the hour-glass or the menacing pinchbeck of the serpents notwithstanding, expressed mendacity rather than triumph. "Death is expiated by living." A beggar from whom alms are begged. As for the Devil, he was as weary as the rest, too horribly demonic to be wholly credible. A wild alibi in the lives of men, so much so that there were moves afoot at that very moment to restore to him all his lost vigour: theological assault therapies, philosophical reanimation techniques, para-psychological and metaphyschic practices. But the Devil was tired enough to be content to leave it all to mankind, who could manage everything better than him. And the Knight: where was he bound for, armed from head to toe, so unshakeable of purpose, dragging behind him that weary figure of the Devil, and so hastily refusing Death charity? Would he ever struggle up to the walled citadel on high, the citadel of the supreme truth, of the supreme lie?

Christ? Savonarola? No, no, far from it. Perhaps what Dürer had placed inside that armour was the real death, the real devil: and it was life which, with that armour and those weapons, believed itself secure in itself.

Wrapped up in these thoughts, themselves affected by a strain of incandescent delirium, he had almost dozed off: the Chief, who came bursting into his office, found him in that state and said: "You really are unwell." Since he had become aware that the Deputy was failing and in pain, the Chief no longer sent for him when he had to talk to him: a kindness that the Deputy appreciated, but not without an element of annoyance.

"Not as much as I would like to be," replied the Deputy, shaking himself awake, but feeling his pain reawaken too.

"What are you saying?" the Chief replied, pretending to be scandalised, but having understood perfectly well that the point the other wished to reach in feeling unwell was the point where he would feel no pain at all. However he was too blissfully happy to be side-tracked by anyone else's problems: "Have you heard? What do you think?"

"Undoubtedly," said the Deputy, with measured and gleeful malice, "he deserves some punishment for what he has got up to: a charge, as well the obvious one of self-calumny, of giving misleading information, of conduct likely to provoke a breach of the peace ..."

"What do you mean?" This time not pronounced formally, but as a cry from the soul.

"I mean what I have meant from the very beginning: if we go along with this game of the Children of Eighty-nine, if we give a hand in creating them, this story will have no end; there'll be victims one after the other, and I do not just mean in the form of the corpses of murder victims, I mean people like the one you have in your clutches right now."

"What do you mean?" once more, but this time heartfelt and almost imploring: "What we have in our hands is a vital link in the chain, and you want us to toss it away as if it were worthless."

"You're quite right: a link in a chain, but it is a chain of stupidity and human suffering, a chain of a quite different sort from what you have in mind. Be patient, listen to me for a moment ... This boy will carry on denying today, maybe even tomorrow, for a whole week, let's say for a month: but the day will come when he will confess to being a member of a subversive, revolutionary association called the Children of Eighty-nine. He will declare himself ready, no ... desperate to collaborate and, with our assistance, will provide the names of one, two, three accomplices, fellow members ... I wonder if he'll choose from those of his acquaintance he likes most or least; that's a psychological mechanism that would repay study, don't you think? ... In any case, we'll soon have further links in our chain ... By this time – you don't need much imagination to picture it – the police force will be out and about talking to professors, janitors, barmen, disco owners, managers of takeaway sandwich stalls – a new word, that ... it makes me tremble all over ... as though they had stuck together sandwiches and book stalls – Anyway, there they are busily interrogating, with the aim of getting as many names as possible of the people this young man saw regularly – in the unlikely event of his obstinately refusing to talk, of his refusing to provide names, we would have no problem in picking one or two names at random from the list which will emerge from these enquiries ..."

"You really are unwell," he said in a concerned, persuasive tone: "Take a holiday: a couple of months off. You're due it: I'll see to it right away, if you like."

"Thank you. I'll think it over."

TEN

"Morphine is wonderful: it is essential to take it when you can't stand it any more," a medical friend had advised him, handing over a little packet. The effects of a morphine dose were wonderful, more so when they succeeded an intolerable level of pain. The stronger the storm the greater the peace. "Peace after the Storm", "Saturday in the Village", "The Solitary Sparrow", "Infinity": Giacomo Leopardi, that poet happy in his unhappiness. What great and profound sentiments, expressed with utter simplicity and even with banal images had he revealed and stamped indelibly on the memory of that generation of Italians who could now be called ageing: in their far-off school years, and thereafter. Did they still read him nowadays in school? Maybe so, but there was certainly no child who knew his poems by heart. *Par coeur*, as the French teacher would put it, distributing the poems of Victor Hugo, almost invariably Victor Hugo. He could call them to mind even now:

> *Devant la blanche ferme où parfois vers midi*
> *Un vieillard vient s'asseoir sur le seuil attiédi ...*

> *Oh! combien de marins, combien de capitaines*
> *Qui sont partis joyeux pour des courses lontaines*
> *Dans ce morne horizon se sont évanouis ...*

And he had them even more par coeur now. The sheer beauty of the expression, which he translated "in the heart, from the heart and for the heart". He discovered himself sentimental to

59

the point of tears. But the doctor, with that sybilline, contra-dictory phrase, had only intended to warn him against dependency.

But what was the point at which a person just could not stand it any more? He pushed it further and further into the future, like some finishing-post in a contest between the will and pain. And not out of any fear of dependency, but from a sense of dignity in which the mere fact of his having been for the greater part of his life an upholder of the law, and of its proscriptions and prohibitions, played a part. He was well aware of what morphine was in a pharmacopoeia, in a hospi-tal, in a doctor's bag or at the bedside of someone who had arrived at the point of being unable to take any more. Still, he could not quite bring himself to view it in the sunlight of permitted things, removed from the shadow of transgression and crime in which he, after years of practice, had been accus-tomed to considering it. The law. A law, he thought, how-ever iniquitous, is still a form of reason: to obtain the objective of extreme, definitive iniquity the very people who willed and framed the law must themselves distort it and do it violence. Fascism was, among other things, this: a constant evasion of its own laws. So too was Stalin's communism – even more so.

And the death penalty? But the death penalty has nothing to do with the law: it is an act of self-consecration to crime, of the consecration of crime. A community will always, by a majority, proclaim the need for the death penalty, precisely because it is a consecration. The sacred, whatever it had to do with the sacred ... The dark pit of being, of existence.

Morphine, then. And a curious thought, prompted by curi-osity, occurred to him: he wondered if in the year in which Tolstoy set the death of Ivan Ilich the use of morphine, for that purpose, was already known. 1885, 1886? It was reason-able to assume it was known, but was there any reference to it in the story? He thought not, and drew a kind of comfort from that reflection. Tolstoy was motivated by perhaps the

same considerations as he was in refusing his character morphine. Thinking over that short story, he began to search
inside himself for comparisons. Death as a quidditas, a quan-
tum which coursed in the blood among bones, muscles and
glands, until it found the niche, cradle or little cavity in which
to explode. A minuscule explosion, a point of fire, an ember
initially flickering, then of constant, penetrating pain: and it
grew and it grew until, having reached the point where the
body no longer seemed able to contain it, it overflowed into
everything around. Only the mind, with its tiny, momentary
victories, was its enemy, but there were moments, interminably long moments, when pain fell on every single thing,
darkening and deforming everything. It fell on every pleasure
which remained within reach – on love itself, on well-loved
pages, on happy memories. Because it took possession of the
past, too, as though it had always been present, as though
there never had been a time when it was not there, when the
body was healthy, young and given over to joy, in joy.
Something resembling a satanic inversion of inflation was
under way: those tiny reserves of joy which had been successfully put aside in the course of a life were being malevolently
devoured by that pain. On the other hand, perhaps everything
in the world took place under the sign of inflation; everyday
the currency of life was losing its value: all life was a kind of
empty, monetary euphoria bereft of purchasing power. The
gold standard – of emotions, of thought – had been pillaged:
the things of real value had now an unaffordable, if not
wholly unknown, price.

Without having really decided, he was embarked on a
search to check what was left of his personal reserves. He was
walking along the banks of the river, stopping every so often
to look at the muddy water, to watch life and time flow by.

He arrived at her house worn out: only one flight of stairs,
of old stairs with low, smooth steps, but for him every ascent
was now an exertion. Strangely, though, the exertion chased
away the pain. He decided he must discuss it with a doctor;

for all he knew there existed an exertion therapy; these days they discover so many, grow tried of them, rediscover them, only to grow tired of them all over again. The fact is that just as nature, with precious few elements at her disposal, is capable of forging an infinity of different faces, so it is, obscurely, with the intestines. What can a doctor know about all that? Even when there is the will to communicate to him that little which each of us feels – of the heart, of the lungs, of the stomach, of the bones – a doctor has no option but to refer it all to abstractions, to universals: even when everything is reported to him with the greatest of precision, like Proust in the dentist's waiting-room describing his toothache to Roditi, giving Roditi the consolation of discovering his own to be identical.

He rang the doorbell: carillon notes in the distance; something which always upset him, but more so now than ever. As usual, she came to the door a few minutes later, in the dressing-gown which, he was fully aware, she had slipped on that very minute. *Mais n'te promènes donc pas toute nue ... Never walk about completely naked.* He remembered, many years previously, in a small theatre in Rome (in Via Santo Stefano del Cacco, alongside both his office and that of Inspector Ingravallo, familiarly known as Don Ciccio Ingravallo; because such was the truth of the pages of Gadda's novel that he had the impression of having bumped into him on those offices rather than on the printed page), having seen Franca Rame walk about the stage, certainly not naked, and clad in a nightdress which was anything but transparent: because in those days transparent attire, let alone nudity, could provide one of his colleagues with the justification for girding himself in the tricolour sash and having the curtain brought down in any theatre. No longer: today clothes are removed without a second thought, in the theatre as in reality; and to think that in his childhood taking off one's clothes was considered the height of madness. "He stripped himself bare naked": reason enough, if anyone appeared in that state, for the strait-jacket, the doctor's surgery, the asylum.

At home she walked about completely naked, to the delight, no doubt, as in Feydeau's farce, of the people in the building opposite, but causing him moments of searing jealousy. Inside himself, now, he laughed at it, and so a sketch featuring the De Rege brothers (the theatre again) flashed into his mind. One of them came on limping with his head bandaged, his arm in plaster, blaming it all, it seemed, on "jealousy". The dialogue between the two went back and forth on the subject of the wife's jealousy until it became clear, in the course of the conversation, that those injuries were not the effect of an emotional spasm but of a fall from a *gelosia*, that is a shutter, a window shade ... the same word which also denoted jealousy. It may even be that the window attachment had been first dreamed up to ward off the tormented emotion of the same name, but the two had now nothing at all in common. It seemed that the emotion had been abolished in recent years, although possibly it was now making a come-back, but stripped of the overtones of tragedy: more redolent of ascetic preoccupations.

In the midst of these thoughts, which hardly deserved the name of thought, fleeting and pell-mell as they were, her amazement and momentary hesitation before recognising him caused him to see himself as though reflected in a mirror. The image, irrationally, irritated him profoundly, as though she had gone into her one of her, once adorable, little huffs. It lasted, like the regret for having returned to visit her at all, the merest moment.

"At long last," she said. "Where have you come from, what have you been doing all these months?"

"I was in Switzerland: didn't you get my letter?"

"A postcard," she corrected him angrily.

"That's right, a card ... and this last couple of days in the office, I've been snowed under with work."

"The Children of Eighty-nine?"

"The Children of Eighty-nine, among other things."

"And this business in Switzerland?"

"A medical check-up. Very gruelling."

"And what came out of it . . ."

"All clear."

He could see from her eyes that she did not believe in that medical all clear, but she had the shrewdness, the delicacy, the love perhaps, not to insist. She began to talk ramblingly about other things, but only about what had been happening to her during the period when they had not seen each other. She uttered no reproaches over his absence or his silence.

He stared at her, guessing at that familiar body underneath the flimsy clothing, that body he had loved and desired for years, never more than when she began to feel her youth passing and her body fading. Then she had felt herself menaced and offended, as though by an injustice or a criminal assault. At the same time there grew in him a feeling of tenderness which nourished and sharpened his desire. Desire and tenderness: all serene after the passion of the early years when their meetings were filled with problems and occasioned misunderstandings and resentments, from which pain and despair rose up like hurricanes. However, once the problems were ended, the passion was spent. Gone were those obsessions and agonies which she perhaps enjoyed but which he lived like one of those fevers where the rise and fall of temperature, of delirium and lucidity, mark the passage of days and hours. They always met with joy – the joy of their bodies, the only sort of which they could be mutually convinced; there was no need to ask more; they travelled together, at times undertaking journeys of unplanned variety and duration, although ever less frequently of late. Everything withdrew, everything was now far off. There remained in him that feeling of tenderness, now almost transformed into pity. Odd how in him now, every feeling which had been love or dislike was changed to pity. And even more odd how memory transfigured those far-off sufferings and depairs into beauty. Everything lied, memory included.

"What about these Children of Eighty-nine?"

"Somebody felt they were necessary." Dürer's devil from the print came to mind. "There has to be a devil before there can be holy water."

ELEVEN

"You seem more at peace," said the Chief.

"Oh, as to peace ... as regards what is happening inside here, I would rather say that I have reached a state of indifference ... Forgive me if I speak to you in this way, with the sincerity of two equals: you are my direct superior and ...."

"Don't say that. I have always treated you as a friend, and I am aware of what is going on inside you, of your pain ... And as a friend, I want to put a clear, direct question to you: what do you want? From me, from us, from everybody involved in tackling this case."

"Not a thing. At this point, nothing at all. I see quite clearly that things can only go in the direction they are going, and that it is impossible not just to turn back, but even to stop."

"Tell me the truth: you wanted a warrant for Aurispa's arrest." The fact that he now called him Aurispa and no longer the President was, none the less, a sign that he too felt, equally ardently, the same futile desire – to see a warrant issued for the arrest of Aurispa.

"Look: any time, in other places, thank God not in this one any longer ... any time I have had to execute warrants, I always felt like one of those sinister characters who – you remember the Stations of the Cross in country villages? – crept up to take Christ prisoner. No matter how vile the person to be arrested was, my state of mind was always the same ... Yes, it was necessary to execute the warrant: often, if by no means always, it was right; but I could never manage to get over that sensation."

66

"It's a feeling which does you credit. But in our job ... forgive me for asking this, but why didn't you become a lawyer instead of a policeman?"

"Perhaps because I deluded myself that you could best be a lawyer by being a policeman ... Just take that as a joke. It's not true. People lie constantly, we do nothing but lie ... to ourselves more than to anybody else ... Anyway, no, I was not looking for a warrant for Aurispa's arrest, but I did want us to concentrate a little more on him, on his life and interests. And, more than anything else, I would have preferred us to pack that putative Child of Eighty-nine off home ... Where is he now, by the way? In isolation, I presume, in a cell two metres by three."

"What do you expect?"

"Between friends, if you will allow me ... in all sincerity ... do you really believe that that boy has any part in some terrorist group which made its debut with the murder of Sandoz?"

"I wouldn't take an oath on it, but in the normal run of things ..."

"In the abnormal run of things," the Deputy corrected him. To bring this useless discussion to an end, he went on: "I took your advice. I handed in a request for a period of leave. For two months. I think that will be sufficient."

"Sufficient for what?" asked the Chief, all ready with words of comfort and encouragement.

"To get my health back. What else?"

He went over to his office, opened the drawers of his desk and took out some letters, a packet of cigarettes and Gide's pocket edition of Montaigne, which he knew almost by heart. He left other cigarettes and other books. He stopped in front of the Dürer, uncertain whether to take it or leave it. He decided to leave it, indulging, with some relish, a fantasy over what would become of it. He imagined his successors regarding it as part of the furnishing of that office, like the map of the city and the portrait of the President of the Republic. Then someone would become aware of its status as Res Nullius, would carry it triumphantly home or, possibly, to an bric-à-brac stall, where a dealer would discover it and the whole itinerary by which things end up at nearly chic auction sales would be underway all over again. At least in this way it would come to the attention of lovers of such things, or to one lover, someone like him, perhaps; an extemporised, incompetent lover.

He strolled around the city, relishing a sense of freedom which he never remembered experiencing before. Life retained all its beauty, but only for those who were still worthy of it. He felt himself to be not unworthy, indeed to be almost among the selected. It was time to cry out: "God hath given you one face, and you make yourselves another": not in the spirit of Hamlet to women, with their cosmetics, face-creams or lipsticks, but to all who merited the tag "unworthy", to the whole worthless mass who were multiplying day by day and filling the earth. He burned with the wish to bellow to the world that this was its new essence – that it had shown itself unworthy of life. But had not the world, the human world, always obscurely aspired to being unworthy of life? An ingenious and ferocious enemy of life, of itself, while at the same time the inventor of so many benevolent forces – law, rules of play, proportions, symmetries, fictions, good manners ... "The ingenious enemy of myself", the dramatist Vittorio Alfieri had said of himself, of himself the man; but equally the ingenious friend, at least until yesterday. As usual, however, when he arrived at the misery of today and the despair of tomorrow, he wondered whether in deploring the indignity into which the world was sinking there was not an element of rancour at being about to die, and of envy towards those who would remain. Perhaps it was so, even in the midst of the all-embracing pity he felt for those who would remain: so much so that at certain moments, embittered, he found himself repeating to himself, like the compères of Variety shows in his younger days, a

"Have a wonderful time, ladies and gentlemen": like a farewell greeting, scoffingly. None the less, in the awareness that there would be no "Wonderful time", there was, however perversely, a hint of pity.

He was now walking through the park. The children, yes, the children: so graceful, so much better fed than previously (the frail and hungry childhood of those who were now elderly), perhaps more intelligent and undoubtedly, overall, better informed: yet he had for them an enormous compassion and apprehension. Will they still be here in 1999, in 2009 or in 2019, and what would this succession of decades bring them? Immersed in these thoughts, he realised he had reached, as it were, the threshold of prayer, which he glimpsed as a deserted, desolate garden.

He stopped to follow their games, to eavesdrop on what they were saying to each other. They were still capable of joy, of imagination, but lying in wait for them was a school without joy and without imagination, the television, the computer, the car from home to school and from school to home, and food which was rich but as tasteless as blotting paper. Never again, committed to memory, the multiplication tables, the poems ... "The maiden from the country came..." or else "All trembling on the threshold ..." or even "The cypresses which at Bolgheri ..." – torments of other times. Memory was to be abolished, all Memory; and similarly those exercises which aimed at making it flexible, subtle or retentive.

In the small towns, children could still enjoy the same freedom as before, but in the cities everything, by necessity and science, was like a battery-hen farm. Some were intent on having them born as monsters, perhaps prodigious monsters, for a monstrous world. "What we are doing," a famous physicist had once told him, "is all flowers and roses compared to the things biologists are up to." He was somewhat confused by the expression "flowers and roses", as though the rose, by virtue of literature, had been separated from the genre "flower". The roses I failed to pluck, he thought to himself. But it was not true, it is not true that life is made up of missed opportunities. No regrets.

A dog, an Alsatian with a good-natured, worn-out appearance, had approached a pram in which a fair-haired baby was peacefully asleep. The girl who was supposedly looking after the child was engaged in a conversation with a soldier. On an impulse he went over and positioned himself between the dog and the pram. The girl left off talking to the soldier, threw him a reassuring smile and, gazing affectionately in the direction of the dog, said it was an old, friendly thing which would never harm a living soul. He continued on his way and, noticing how many dogs were roaming around the park, attempted to count them. So many dogs, perhaps even more than the multitudes of children. What if the slaves were to count themselves, Seneca had once asked. Supposing the dogs were to count themselves? There had one day appeared among his routine cases the horror of a child savaged by a Great Dane. The family pet: no doubt old, friendly and never harming a living soul, just like the girl's Alsatian. Looking round at the many children running through the park, and at the countless dogs which seemed to be running alongside them or watching over them as they played, that case from long ago came back to mind and brought an apocalyptic vision. He could feel it on his face like an unclean, clinging spider's web of images. He lifted his hand to wipe it off, warning himself to die better. The dogs were still there, too many of them; they had nothing in common with those which, his father being an avid hunter, had been around him in his childhood. Small dogs, those, a pack of squat, Sicilian mongrels; always playful, tails wagging, filled with a love of the countryside rather than of the hunt. These dogs, on the other hand, were enormous, doleful creatures, their minds seemingly set on thick, dark woods or impenetrable stone quarries. Or Nazi concentration camps. In any case, for anyone who gave it any thought, it was clear there were too

many of them everywhere. And too many cats. And mice
What if they were to count themselves?

That obsession fading, he passed from one thought to the
next and began to recall the dogs of his childhood, their
names, the prowess of some, the laziness of others – in the
very way that his father had talked about them in conversation with fellow hunters. A thought which had never previously occurred to him now suddenly flashed into his mind:
not one of them had died at home. None of them had been
seen dying or found dead in their basket of straw and old
blankets. At a certain stage in life, or at a certain stage in the
progress of their bronchitis, it had been noted that they had
no further taste for food or play, and they simply disappeared.
The shame of themselves dead. As in Montaigne. And the
fact, asserted almost as the Kantian imperative, as an illus-
tration of that imperative, that one of mankind's highest
intelligences, in his wish that death should come to him,
preferably in solitude but at least far away from those who
had been close to him in life, had by meditation and reasoning
attained what the dogs instinctively felt, seemed to him sublime. This train of thought, mediated by the great shadow of
Montaigne, succeeded in reconciling him with the dogs.

TWELVE

After one of his more peaceful nights, with pain awakening him at the end of dreams in which something or someone seemed to be continually beating him on the side, on the shoulder or on the neck, he passed the following morning with his newspapers, magazines and books. The Great Journalist had written an article in which he bitterly accused the police and security services of having fostered the re-emergence of the cancer of terrorism, and of having realised what had happened only when they were confronted with the corpse of poor Sandoz in the morgue. The Catholic journal, *The Pilgrim*, published a lengthy article dealing with the wickedness of the '89 and of these its blessèd offspring of today. They were not exactly called blessèd in the article, but since they were engaged in killing, a certain measure of understanding and indulgence, in anticipation of final forgiveness, had to be afforded them.

The pain appeared to be dimmed and to have taken on the semblance of a milky, off-white substance. He finished re-reading *Treasure Island*, which still resembled happiness. He was on the point of replacing it on his bookshelf when the woman who came every morning to tidy up what little that there was to tidy up arrived. She had not expected to find him at home, and asked if he were not well or if he had decided to take a break.

"A break, a short break."

"Good for you," she said: there had been, in the course of the morning, a murder, something really big. It was not hard to imagine how busy the police would be.

He asked about the murder as he rushed over to switch on the radio. The woman said that the victim was a friend of the man who had been killed a week ago, but she could not remember his name.

There was not, in all the hubbub of music and chatter which the radio dispensed, a single voice giving any news. He switched it off.

To make up for the silence of the radio on the murder, the woman did her best to remember.

"It was the name of a town in Southern Italy."

"Rieti?"

"Yes, that's it, Rieti." The woman brightened up at the recollection. She thought to herself: these people know everything that is going to happen before it does. She too, although proud of her Northern origins and not from Southern Italy, was harsh in her judgements on the police.

A friend of the man who had been killed a week previously, the name of a town in Southern Italy: the name Rieti had immediately occurred to him. Now more than pain, stronger than pain, a feeling of defeat overcame him. He felt as though entangled in one of those detective stores where the author, without warning, uses and abuses the reader, with crass duplicity which never even manages to be clever. Except that, in this case, the duplicity was a mistake, a mistake of his. Had it possibly also been a mistake of Rieti's? Or had Rieti hidden that part of the factual truth in which he was most directly interested?

He spent hours turning it over in his mind, as though engaged in an endless game of patience in which something always went awry: one card which refused to be fitted into place, one space into which the awkward card could not be placed.

He left his house as night, mixed with fog, was falling. He headed, without having decided on it – like a donkey for the stables, he thought when he noticed what he was doing – for the office.

He heard the shots, or so it seemed to him, an incommensurable time before feeling himself hit. He fell thinking: you fall as a precaution and as a convention. He believed he could rise to his feet, but found himself unable to. He raised himself on an elbow. Life was draining out of him, effortlessly, in a flow: the pain was no more. The hell with morphine, he thought. Everything was clear, now: Rieti had been murdered because he had spoken to him. At what point had they started following him?

His elbow had no longer the strength to support him and he fell back. He saw the lovely, immobile face of Signora Zorni light up with malice. He watched it fade away, at the end of the time whose threshold he was even now crossing, into the headlines of the following day's papers:

CHILDREN OF EIGHTY-NINE STRIKE AGAIN.
COLD-BLOODED MURDER OF INVESTIGATING OFFICER.

He thought: what confusion! But it was now, eternally and ineffably, the thought of the mind into which his own had dissolved.

A Straightforward Tale

TRANSLATED BY JOSEPH FARRELL

Yet again my purpose is to examine scrupulously the possibilities even now afforded to justice.

DURRENMATT, *Justice*

ONE

The phone call came at 9:37 on the evening of the 18 March, a Saturday, the eve of the refulgent, rumbustious festivities which the city dedicated to St Joseph the Carpenter: in honour of the Carpenter bonfires of unwanted articles of furniture were lit in the working-class areas of the city, like a pledge to those few carpenters still in business that there would be no shortage of work for them. All over the city, offices were even more deserted than was normal at that hour. Even if the offices in the police station were still a blaze of light, their late evening and all-night illumination was no more than a tacitly agreed sop to the citizenry, giving the impression that their security was the constant concern of the people employed in those offices.

The switchboard operator noted the hour and the name of the person making the call – Giorgio Roccella. He had a cultured, calm, persuasive voice. "Like all cranks," thought the operator. Signor Roccella asked to speak to the Chief Superintendent, no less: sheer madness, especially at that time, and on that evening of all evenings.

The operator made an effort to adopt the same tone, but managed only a jeering imitation, made all the more obvious by the brusqueness of his words: "The Chief Superintendent is never in the police station at this hour." The brusqueness reflected the attitude current in the office on the subject of the Chief Superintendent's frequent absences. "I'll put you on to the Inspector," he added, with a delight at riling the Inspector, who would undoubtedly be on his way out at that very moment.

The Inspector was indeed getting into his overcoat. The sergeant, whose desk was at right angles to the Inspector's, picked up the phone. He listened, rummaging about on the desk for pencil and paper, and, as he wrote, he replied yes, they would be there as soon as possible, just as soon as humanly possible, but choosing words which indicated that possibility and swiftness did not necessarily coincide.

"Who was that?" asked the Inspector.

"Somebody or other who says he has to show us right away a thing he has found in his house."

"A body?" joked the Inspector.

"No, his exact words were – a thing."

"A thing . . . and does this somebody have a name?"

The sergeant picked up the notepad on which he had scribbled name and address: "Giorgio Roccella, in Cotugno; four kilometres from where the road to Monterosso forks to the right; that makes fifteen from here."

The Inspector turned back from the door to the sergeant's desk, picked up the notepad, peered at it as though convinced he would uncover something more than the sergeant had read out. He said:

"Can't be."

"What can't be?" asked the sergeant.

"This Roccella," said the Inspector, "he's a diplomat, a consul or ambassador somewhere or other. He hasn't been here for years. He closed up his house in the city and let his cottage in the country the road. It's on a hill-top, more like a mini-fortress."

"The old farmhouse," said the sergeant, "I've passed it dozens of times."

"Inside the compound, which is what makes it look like a farmhouse, there's a beautiful little villa . . . or at least, there used to be . . . A big family, the Roccellas, but the only one left is this consul or ambassador or whatever he is . . . I didn't even know he was still alive. It's so long since he's been around."

"If you like," said the sergeant, "I'll go and have a look."

"No need, I'm sure it's only a hoax. Tomorrow, if you've the time and the inclination, drop by and check up that everything is all right. As far as I am concerned, whatever happens, don't come looking for me tomorrow. I'll be celebrating St Joseph's with some friends at their place in the country."

TWO

The following day the sergeant set off for Cotugno, and both
he and the two officers accompanying him were in the high
spirits of people off for a day out. From what the Inspector
had said, they were sure that the place was uninhabited and
that the call the evening before was no more than a hoax. A
stream which had once run at the foot of the hill was now no
more than a pebbly river bed, lined with stones as white as
bones, but the hill leading up to the ruined farmhouse was
covered with green foliage. Their plan was to carry out a
swift search of the house and then, in a more festive mood, to
start gathering asparagus and chicory. All three, like the good
peasants they were, prided themselves on their skill in identifying the best wild herbs.

They got inside the enclosure, which was not made up, as
might have seemed from the road below, of ordinary walls
but of outhouses. The doors were secured by shining locks,
and the buildings were grouped in a circle around the little
villa. The villa was indeed a jewel, even if it now showed
signs of decay and dilapidation. All the shutters were closed
except for one, which allowed them to peer inside. The bright
light of that March morning afforded them at first only a
confused glimpse of the interior. Gradually they managed to
make things out, and as all three, shielding their eyes from the
sun with their hands, repeated the exercise, it became clear
that a man, his back towards them, lay slumped over the desk
where he had been sitting.

The sergeant took the decision to break the glass, open the
window and enter the room: the man might have taken

unwell and possibly they were in time to offer assistance. But the man was dead, and not from any stroke or heart attack: in the head, which rested on the surface of the desk, a clot of blackish blood had formed between the lower jaw and the temple.

The sergeant shouted to the two officers who had climbed over the window-sill after him – "Don't touch a thing!" To avoid touching the phone, which was on the desk, he ordered one of the officers to return to the police station, make a report and dispatch at once a doctor, a photographer and those two or three officers in the station who had a reputation, and the accompanying privileges, for scientific expertise. Unwarranted privileges, in the sergeant's view, for he had yet to see a single case where their contribution had been helpful rather than the reverse.

Having issued these orders, and all the while repeating to the officer who has stayed with him not to touch anything, the sergeant began his inspection. He was deeply conscious of the written report which it would be his duty, in due course, to file, and this task invariably weighed heavily with him, for his years at school and his lack of reading had done little to instil in him much confidence over the use of Italian. But, curiously, the fact of being compelled to write about the things he had seen, and the worry and near panic involved, gave his mind such a capacity for choice, for selectivity, for identifying the essential detail, that what eventually emerged in written form was invariably penetrating and judicious. Perhaps it is so for all writers from the South of Italy, and from Sicily in particular – high school, university and wide reading notwithstanding.

The immediate impression was that the man had committed suicide. The pistol was on the ground, to the right of the chair on which he was seated: an old weapon, German, dating from the 1915–18 war, the sort of thing survivors would bring home with them as souvenirs. But there was one detail which cancelled out that first impression in the sergeant's mind: the right hand of the dead man, which ought to have been hanging limply over the fallen pistol, was instead resting on the top of the desk, holding steady a sheet of paper on which was written ... "I have found." That full stop after the word "found' burned into the darkness like a flash-bulb, lighting up, swiftly and fleetingly, the murder scene which lay behind the imperfectly constructed suicide scene. The man had begun writing "I have found," in the same way he had informed the police that he had found something he had not expected to: unsure whether the police would arrive, and perhaps growing afraid in the silence and solitude, he was about to write down what he had found when a knock came at the door. "The police", he thought to himself, and instead it was the murderer. Perhaps the person introduced himself as a policeman: the man brought him in, sat down again at his desk and began to tell him about his discovery. The pistol might have been lying on the desk; probably, in his growing fear, he had gone to retrieve it from some old hiding place where he remembered leaving it (the sergeant did not believe that the killers would have such an ancient piece of weaponry in their possession). Seeing the gun lying there on the desk, the murderer possibly asked about it, checked that it was still in working order before suddenly pointing it at the man's head and firing. At this point, he had the idea of adding a full stop after the "I have found" ... "I have found that life is not worth living", or "I have found the ultimate and only truth", "I have found, I have found–" everything and nothing. It did not make sense. From the murderer's point of view, however, that full-stop was not wholly a mistake. In support of the suicide hypothesis which would undoubtedly be advanced – the sergeant had absolutely no doubts on that score – all kinds of existential and philosophical significance would be adduced from that full-stop, especially if the personality of the deceased offered the slightest pretext. On the desk there was a bunch of keys, an old pewter inkwell, and a photograph, evidently taken in the garden at least fifty years previously, of a large, happy party of people. Perhaps it had been taken there, outside the window, when there would have been rows of trees creating their own harmony and shade, but where now there was nothing but the untended barrenness of weeds and scrub.

Beside the sheet of paper with the "I have found", lay a fountain-pen with the cap neatly screwed on. A fine flourish, this, by the murderer (the sergeant was becoming more convinced by the second that he was engaged on a murder enquiry) to convey the impression that with the full-stop the man had put a final stop to his own existence.

The room was lined with book-shelves, almost all empty of books. The few works that remained included bound copies of a year's run of legal reviews, some agronomy manuals and random bundles of a magazine entitled *Nature and Art*. Some volumes, which must have been very old, lay piled one on top of the other, and on their spine the sergeant read *Calepinus*. He had always believed that a calepin was a pocket-sized booklet, like a notebook or a handbook, and it struck him as odd that a word more appropriate to miniatures should be applied to great tomes each weighing at least ten kilos. Scruples over not leaving fingerprints, although he had precious little faith in them, made him check his curiosity and leave the volumes unopened. The same scruples caused him, as he wandered around the house followed by the officer, not to touch furniture or handles, and only to enter by doors already open.

The house was much bigger than would have seemed possible from the outside. There was an enormous dining-room with a large oak table and four dressers of the same wood, and inside he found dishes, soup tureens, glasses and coffee-pots, as well as old toys, papers and linen. There were three bedrooms, two with mattresses and pillows stacked on the springs, but the third appeared to have been slept in the previous night; there could have been yet others behind the doors which the sergeant decided not to open. The house had been abandoned and stripped of furnishings, books, paintings and ceramics – there were clear marks where objects had been removed – but did not have the air of being uninhabited. Cigarette stubs filled the ashtrays, and the dregs of wine stained the bottom of the glasses, all five of them, which had been carried into the kitchen, no doubt to be rinsed. The kitchen, complete with wooden fireplace, oven and decorative Valencian tiles on the walls, was spacious; even if they were now turning green with sulphate, the copper pots and pans hanging on the walls conferred, in the uncertain light, a certain splendour on the scene. From the kitchen a low door opened on to a narrow, dark staircase which ascended towards some unseen area.

The sergeant groped around for a stair-light to enable him to see his way. Unable to find any switch except the one for the lamps over the fireplace, he took the risk of climbing the stairs in the dark. After five or six steps, still fumbling forward, he began to strike matches, and had used up several before reaching a kind of attic at the head of the stairs. It was as wide as the dining-room, but was so low-ceilinged that a person of normal height would find it difficult to avoid bumping his head. It was filled with couches, armchairs, broken seats, strongboxes, damaged picture frames and dusty drapes. Ten gilded bust-reliquaries of saints stood around in a circle, but one larger bust with a silver chest, black cape and bulldog features attracted attention. The gilded busts each carried the name of the saint they represented on their baroque pedestals, but the sergeant was not familiar enough with saints to recognize, in the larger and darker bust, the figure of St Ignatius.

The sergeant lit his last match and hurried downstairs. "A stuffy loft packed with saints," he explained to the officer standing waiting for him at the foot of the stairs. He felt as though spider's webs, dust and mildew had fallen on his head. He jumped over the window-sill back into the cool, bright morning, back into the sun and grass glistening with frost.

With the officer the regulation two paces behind him, they

made a tour of the exterior of the house. Among the weeds and undergrowth, there was a clearing which had plainly been used as a turning place for cars and possibly lorries. "There's been a fair bit of traffic here," said the sergeant. Then, pointing them out to the officer, "What do you make of these chains?" he asked. They were used to secure the doors of the barns or stables which circled the house like a fort in a Western.

"They're new," said the officer.

"Good for you," said the sergeant.

THREE

A little more than two hours later, all those who were supposed to arrive, did: Chief Superintendent, Procurator of the Republic, doctor, Chief Superintendent's tame journalist and a squad of officers including the scientific unit, standing on their dignity. In all there were six or seven cars which, even when they had come to a halt, continued to roar, screech and blare their horns, just as they had done when exiting from the city centre, arousing thereby the curiosity not only of the citizens but also of the rival police force, the Carabinieri – and in so doing achieving the very result the Chief Superintendent had so ardently desired to postpone as long as possible. The consequence was that, half an hour later, the Carabinieri Colonel, scowling, furious and desperate to engage – with all due respect – the Chief Superintendent in a quarrel, arrived on the scene. The doors had already been opened up with the keys which had been found lying on the desk, the taking of fingerprints was, somewhat haphazardly, underway, and the body had already been photographed from every conceivable angle. With barely repressed fury, the Colonel said:

"You might at least have kept us informed."

"I beg your pardon," said the Chief Superintendent, "but it all happened so quickly ... a matter of minutes."

"Of course, of course," said the Colonel, ironically.

The gun was lifted by a pencil inserted in the trigger catch, delicately placed on a black cloth and equally delicately wrapped up. "The fingerprints, quickly, don't waste time," said the Chief Superintendent. The dead man's had already been taken. "A worthless chore," he intoned, "but it has to be done."

"Why worthless?" asked the Colonel.

"Suicide," said the Chief Superintendent, solemnly. The words had the effect of persuading the Colonel of the opposing view.

"Excuse me, sir," interrupted the sergeant.

"Anything you have to say can wait for your report ... meantime ..." but he had no idea, meantime, of what to say or do other than repeat, "Suicide, an evident case of suicide."

The sergeant tried again: "Chief Superintendent ..." He wanted to tell him about the phone-call the previous evening, about the full stop after the "I have found", but the Chief Superintendent cut him off.

"We require the report," he said, indicating himself and the Procurator of the Republic. Glancing at his watch, he added, "Early in the afternoon." Addressing the Procurator and the Colonel:

"A straightforward case, no need to make too much of it ... should be all tied up in no time ... Off you go and write it up right away." Instead, quite automatically, the Colonel saw it shaping up as a very complicated business, as something which would not be tied up "in no time". The unbridgeable disparity of standpoint between the two institutions – the Carabinieri service and the police force – came to the surface immediately, instinctively, as was invariably the case, independently of the individuals who represented them. A long history of rivalry separated them, and any citizen who became entangled with it inevitably ended up as grist to the mill.

The sergeant said: "Yes, sir," and went out to get into the patrol vehicle which had brought him there, only to find it had gone off. Since the Chief Superintendent had upset him, and since he was almost entirely bereft of what is normally called *esprit de corps* – in other words, of the propensity to regard the body to which one belongs as the greater part of any whole, to consider it infallible or, in the event of its showing itself fallible, untouchable, and as always in the right even when it was wrong – a quite outlandish idea occurred to him.

His counterpart, the Carabinieri sergeant, was seated at the wheel of the Colonel's car. Knowing him fairly well, although not to the point of sharing confidences with him, our sergeant went over and sat beside him. He poured out to him all he knew about the case, detailing the various suspicions he harboured. He even pointed out the shining new chains on the doors of the outhouses, and, that task completed, set off in a more cheerful frame of mind for the office, where he devoted over two hours to setting down in writing the things he had explained to his fellow officer in five minutes.

In this way, on the way back into the city, the Carabinieri Colonel learned from his sergeant all he needed to make the case more complex than the Chief Superintendent wished.

FOUR

Although it was Sunday and the feast of St Joseph, data on personal history and family property, together with a host of other more or less confidential pieces of information, flowed both into the Police station and the Carabinieri headquarters; the same data, or almost, from the same sources and the same informers. Had they been able to work harmoniously together, one or other of the parties would have been spared time and effort which could have been more profitably expended in other directions; but now we are yearning for something as impossible as collaboration between a builder and a dynamiter – and let it be clearly understood that neither role is being assigned to either of the two sides in question.

Identity of the victim: Giorgio Roccella from Monterosso, born in Monterosso itself on 14 January 1923, a retired diplomat. He had been Italian consul in various European cities before being sent to Edinburgh where, having separated from his wife, he and his twenty-year-old son still resided. For the past fifteen years he had not set foot in Italy, returning only to die in such tragic circumstances on 18 March 1989. Even if he took little care of it, he was the only member of the family to retain some fragment of what had been a vast and varied estate: all that remained was a semi-derelict house in town and that little villa with its small surrounding plot. He had arrived in town that very day, 18 March; having lunched at the Tre Candele restaurant on spaghetti in cuttlefish sauce and octopus with salad, he called a taxi to take him to the villa. He had, according to the taxi-driver, made sure that his keys opened the doors before allowing him to go, but he gave him orders to return the following day at eleven o'clock. "I am prone to insomnia," he explained, "and will work through the night." The following morning at eleven o'clock, the taxi-driver, seeing the bustle of police and Carabinieri, had turned back without going up to the villa. Perhaps, he thought to himself, the man is a dangerous criminal. Why go looking for trouble?

The Chief Superintendent, already more than sufficiently irritated by the sergeant's report, which hinted at murder, found in the discovery that the man had separated from his wife (or, preferably, his wife from him) grounds for reinforcing his own belief in the suicide hypothesis. He did wonder why he had gone to the trouble of first calling the police, but the question did not cause him any anxiety. He wanted, he replied, to kill himself under the very eyes of the police force, and so ensure maximum impact and originality for his gesture. The sergeant, studying the official forms more attentively, pointed out to the Chief Superintendent that the separation has occurred some twelve years previously. Whatever heart-break it might have occasioned, it was hard to imagine its coming to a peak of despair twelve years after the event. The Chief Superintendent, however, reached his own peak of irritation with the sergeant there and then. "How dare you address such remarks to a superior officer?" he said. "Go and find the Inspector at once, wherever he is."

FIVE

The Inspector, precisely as he had promised on the Saturday, remained imcommunicado until the following Monday morning. At eight o'clock on the dot, complete with hat, overcoat and heavy gloves, wrapped about with a scarf which covered even his mouth, he made his entry into the office. He removed these articles of clothing one by one, shivering continually as he did so. "It's just about as cold inside as out. If there were any birds in here, they'd drop dead with the cold."

He had learned about the weekend's events from the radio and newspapers. He scanned without comment the outline report prepared by the sergeant, and hurried out to confer with the Chief Superintendent.

On his return, he gave every impression of being at daggers drawn with the sergeant. "Enough of your clever tales, eh?" But the clever tales were already in the air. Two hours later, Professor Carmelo Franzo, an old friend of the victim, was seated in the office giving them further sustenance. He told how on Saturday 18 March he had seen Giorgio Roccella arrive out of the blue at his house. Explanation of that surprise journey: he had remembered that in a chest which must have been left in the attic of the villa there were bundles of old letters: one from Garibaldi to his great-grandfather, another from Pirandello to his grandfather (they had been at high school together). Acting on an impulse, he had decided to pick them up and do some work on them. He asked him to accompany him to the villa in the afternoon, but the professor had a regular, pre-arranged dialysis session that very afternoon: to miss the appointment meant days of painful

93

immobility. Otherwise he would have been delighted to go back to the villa after all those years and give a hand in the search. After making an arrangement to meet the following day, Sunday, they parted, but on Sunday evening the news of his friend's death came over the radio.

However, the professor had further, vitally important, information to add. On Saturday evening, a phone-call had come from his friend. He was phoning from the villa, and his first words were: "I had no idea they'd put a phone in." Then he said that while searching for the letters, he had found . . . the very words . . . he had found the famous painting. "Which painting?" the professor had asked him. "The one which went missing a couple of years ago, don't you remember?" The professor was not clear which one he was referring to, but advised him to call the police.

"What a complicated story," said the Inspector, with a mixture of concern and disbelief. "The telephone, the picture; two things Signor Roccella had just found a moment before talking to you." And, in an even more incredulous tone to the professor: "And you believed all this?"

"I believed him all my life; why should I have changed just the other day?"

Meanwhile, the sergeant picked up the telephone directory, flicked through a couple of pages, cast his eye down the columns and read out aloud: "Roccella, Giorgio, from Monterosso, district of Cotugno, 342260 – it's in the phone book."

"Much obliged," said the Inspector acidly. "It is not the fact that it's there which interests me; I am intrigued by the fact that he was unaware of it."

"Perhaps we could . . ." the sergeant began.

"You could; and you will attend to it at once . . . Go to the office of the telephone company, get all the details of the application, of the date of installation, of bills paid . . . better still, make them give you photocopies of the lot."

Turning to the professor, he went on: "Can we go back to the famous picture: gone missing, turned up at your friend's, and presumably missing once more ... You gave me the impression that you had some notion of the painting your friend was talking about."

"You haven't?" the professor stone-walled.

"No idea," said the Inspector. "I have no interest in painting. God knows how many missing paintings there are in Italy. I have a friend in Rome who specialises in that kind of thing. We could get in touch with him ... but in the meantime, tell me which painting you think we are talking about."

"I am no specialist in stolen works of art," said the professor.

"But you have an opinion of your own."

"The same one you ought to have."

"God Almighty, it's always the same, even with professors."

"Even with police inspectors," the professor replied sourly.

The Inspector restrained himself. Had it been anyone else, he would probably have had him locked up, but Professor Franzo was known and respected by the whole city. Generations of pupils had fond, grateful memories of him. So: "Kindly repeat, as accurately as possible, what your friend said to you in person and on the telephone."

The professor, nervously, so nervously as almost to spell out every syllable, repeated all that had been said.

"You're sure you are not omitting anything?" said the Inspector, getting his own back.

"I have an excellent memory, and am not in the habit of omitting things."

"Good, good," said the Inspector, "but just bear in mind that within a short period you will have to repeat everything, word for word, before the judge."

The professor smiled, half pityingly and half sneeringly, but the Chief Superintendent, who had been a student of the professor's, came in at that moment and put an end to the skirmishing.

"Professor, you here?"

"And with an interesting tale to tell," said the Inspector.

The return of the sergeant disturbed the fragile peace. "I've got the request; made three years ago, but with a forged signature . . . the Carabinieri are already on to it."

"Damnation!" shouted the Chief Superintendent, addressing himself to the Carabinieri.

SIX

Now that the professor's evidence had undermined the suicide theory, the police Chief Superintendent, who had originally accepted it, and the Carabinieri Colonel, who had instantly rejected it, each found themselves under pressure from their superiors to get together, clear the air, exchange information, hypotheses and suspicions. They met, so to speak, with clenched teeth, but could not altogether contrive to be entirely vague and inconclusive.

Reconstruction of the event: Signor Roccella, moved by a whim, returned unexpectedly after many years to search for the letters from Pirandello and Garibaldi; he turned up at his friend's house; he dined at the restaurant; he took from his town house, or already had in his possession, the keys of the villa; he travelled out by taxi. There, having ascertained that the keys still worked, he let the taxi driver go and began his search. But what had taken place from that moment on? He had plainly found a telephone installed, but, judging by the professor's report, he did not appear unduly surprised by this discovery. This implied that he had some idea of who was responsible for the installation. On the other hand, the discovery of that painting in the loft, where he had gone to look for the letters, had evidently left him stunned, perhaps even terrified – which explained the telephone calls to his friend and to the police. Since the police did not come immediately he had begun to write – "I have found ..." But, no doubt in a state of fear, he had gone to look out his old Mauser. And in all probability it was just at that moment that he heard a knock at the door. At last, the police. He went to open up; instead it was his murderer.

Points for further enquiry: Had the telephone indeed been installed without his knowledge? Was his return indeed dictated by his desire to repossess the letters from Garibaldi and Pirandello? Had he indeed seen *that* picture or was it simply some old family painting which he had completely forgotten about and which had turned up as he was rummaging about in the loft?

A further, more meticulous search of the villa was called for, but just as they were making up their minds to order one, an event occurred which created intense activity and confusion.

A local train, normally packed with students at that hour – two o'clock in the afternoon – had been stopped at the signals just outside Monterosso. They waited for the signal to change, but half an hour went by and nothing happened.

The railway line ran alongside the main road, and students and railwaymen swarmed on to the highway, liberally cursing the Monterosso station-master, who had plainly either forgotten to clear the line or who had fallen asleep.

There were very few cars on the road at that hour, and only one stopped to ask what was the matter with the train. A Volvo. The engine-driver asked the driver to do him a favour: would he be good enough to drop in at the Monterosso station and wake up the station-master? The Volvo made its way up to the station; they watched it park and then disappear from sight. Evidently it had rejoined the main road by a different side road.

After a while, since the signals remained red, the driver and a group of passengers made their way on foot to the station; a distance of some five hundred metres. They discovered to their horror that the station-master and his assistant were indeed asleep, but a sleep from which there would be no awakening. They had been murdered.

Impartially, both police and Carabinieri were summoned to the scene. Both, instantaneously, gave all their energies to a search for the Volvo man. Their energies were not likely to be stretched, considering that there could not have been more than thirty Volvos in the entire province. The same calculation was made by the Volvo man himself when he learned from the radio that the police were hunting for him. Having no doubt that it could only be a matter of time before they caught up with him, he went to the police station reluctantly and apprehensively, but, as was recorded in the opening words of the official statement, voluntarily.

Name and surname, place and date of birth, residence, profession, previous dealings with the police.

"Not even for a traffic offence," the man said. However, his declaration of profession – representative of a pharmaceuticals company – gave the Inspector the immeasurable delight of being able to adopt a tough tone for the interrogation.

"Do you own a Volvo?"

"Of course."

"Don't say 'of course' when you are replying to my questions ... your Volvo is very expensive."

The man nodded his head.

"Would you include, among the drugs that you sell, things like heroin, cocaine, opium?"

"Listen," said the man, holding back anger and fear, "I came here, of my own free will, with the sole purpose of telling you what I saw yesterday afternoon."

"Then on you go," said the Inspector, in a tone of disbelief.

"I went up to the station, exactly as the train-driver had requested me to do. I knocked at the window of the station-master's office, and he came to the door."

"Who?"

"The station-master, I suppose."

"So you don't know him."

"No. I've already told you what the driver asked me to tell him. I hardly glanced inside the office: there were two other men, and they were rolling up a carpet – I went on my way."

"But by a different road," remarked the Inspector, "and since no one saw you going back down ... Anyway, they were rolling up this carpet."

"The painting," the sergeant let slip.

The Inspector turned a look of anger on him. "Much obliged, but I would have come to that conclusion without your aid."

"Pardon me," said the sergeant, "I would never dare ..." Then ingenuously, with a confused stutter, he added: "You've been to University."

The remark, which sounded sarcastic to the Inspector, drove him into a rage which was directed at the Volvo owner. "I am sorry, but we will have to keep you in custody. We have further enquiries to make."

SEVEN

Sergeant Antonio Lagandara was born in a country village so near to the city as nowadays to be considered part of it. While he was in his final year of a course in economics and business studies, his father – a farm-hand who had risen to become a highly esteemed and much sought after tree-pruner – died in a fall from the top of a cherry-tree which he was stripping of dead branches. Antonio had taken his diploma but, neither having nor finding employment, he joined the police force. Five years later, he received his first promotion. He found the job stimulating, and decided to make a career of it. He enrolled at the Law Faculty, attended lectures as and when he could, and studied hard. A Degree in Law was the supreme ambition, the ultimate dream of his life. The remark which the Inspector had taken amiss was made in all innocence. It plainly still rankled with him when the sergeant returned from escorting the Volvo owner, whose howls of protest echoed round the whole building, down to the cells. "Been to University, eh? ... I can't work out in my mind whether you're really a moron or whether you're just pretending to be ... University! In a country where cinema ushers, waiters and even dustmen have got to have degrees."

"I am very sorry," said the sergeant, sincerely but peevishly.

"Forget it ... I've got an appointment with the Chief Superintendent. Bring along the Volvo man in a quarter of an hour's time."

The Carabinieri Colonel was already in the Chief Superintendent's office, and the Inspector brought them up to date with what had happened. When the Volvo man was brought in by the sergeant, the Chief Superintendent came straight to the point: "So you saw three men in the station-master's office rolling up a carpet, Was there a body inside?"

"A body? No, definitely not."

"How wide was the carpet?"

"Couldn't really say ... perhaps a metre and a half."

"How can you be so sure it was a carpet?" asked the Colonel.

"I never said I was sure of anything ... it looked like a carpet to me."

"Describe it."

"They were rolling up the carpet so that the underside was on top – a rough, unworked, canvas-like material."

"But the underside of a carpet is not like that at all. Is it possible that it was a painting they were rolling up?"

"It's possible, yes."

"Let's move on. There were, you were saying, three men in all."

"That's right, three."

The Chief Superintendent handed him two photographs: "Here's two of them; recognise them?"

They were attempting to lay a trap for him. The man cursed them inwardly. "How could I recognise them? I don't believe I've ever seen these two in my life before."

"Know who they are?" The station-master and his assistant. The people who were murdered."

"But they are not the ones I saw!"

"Didn't you tell us you saw and spoke to the station-master?"

"All right then, it was somebody I took to be the station-master."

"I'm sorry," said the Chief Superintendent, "But I have no option but to hold you in detention for a further period."

The poor devil began anew his howls of protest.

EIGHT

Chief Superintendent, Colonel and Investigating Magistrate met to establish how the enquiries were going. The magistrate assumed an air of deep thought and then said: "Do you know what I think? However unplanned the whole thing may seem, the Volvo man forced his way into the station-master's office, saw the painting, was completely bowled over by it, shot the two men dead and made off with it."

The Chief Superintendent and Colonel exchanged glances of perplexed and ironic disbelief. "You know these instinctive feelings you get about certain characters. I've had one about this Volvo man from the very first, and I very rarely get it wrong with these intuitions of mine. Keep him locked up for me." Since he had to talk to Professor Franzo, he showed them out.

On the way out, the Chief Superintendent muttered: "Dear God!" and the Colonel, "Terrifying!"

The magistrate was already on his feet to welcome his old teacher.

"I can't tell you how glad I am to see you after all these years!"

"All these years, and they're beginning to show," agreed the professor.

"What do you mean? You haven't changed a bit, in your appearance."

"That's more than I can say for you," said the professor, with his customary bluntness.

"This damn work ... but why are you being so formal with me?"

"I always was."

"But even now?"

"I prefer it that way."

"You do remember me?"

"Of course I do."

"Can I ask you one thing ... before we pass on to other matters ... Whenever I had an essay to do, you always gave me three out of ten, because I used to copy. But one day you gave me five. Why?"

"Because you had chosen a more intelligent author to copy from."

The magistrate burst out laughing. "Italian: it was never my best subject. However, as you can see, it was no great drawback. Here I am today, Procurator of the Republic."

"Italian is not Italian: it is training in reasoning," said the professor. "With less Italian, you might have risen higher." The remark was wounding, The magistrate turned pale, and made his interrogation all the tougher.

NINE

The victim's son arrived from Edinburgh, and his wife from Stuttgart, on the same day. The meeting between mother and son was, even for the investigators who had to be present, an unpleasant affair. The wife, quite clearly, had come to see how much of the inheritance she could grab for herself; the son was there in part to prevent her from doing so, but more especially to find out why his father had been killed, and by whom.

The meeting took place in an office in the police station. They did not exchange any form of greeting. The son's first words were: "You can go back to Stuttgart. There's nothing for you here."

"That's your opinion."

"It's not a matter of its being my opinion. It's all laid down in the papers my father lodged in the registry some years ago."

"I am not sure whether those papers are worth much ... anyway they can be challenged. Look, let's sort things out between us. Why don't we sell up and get out?"

"I am not selling. I might even live here. I came back and stayed a long time, many years ago. My grandparents were still alive then. I remember it very well ... we had a lovely time ... yes, perhaps I will stay on. I used to have long conversations with my father about coming back and settling here."

"With your father!" the woman repeated sarcastically.

"Are you trying to say that he was not my father? Look, there is no choosing mothers, or I certainly would never have chosen you ... and by the same token you would never have chosen me as son ... but you can chose your father, and I chose Giorgio. I loved him and I mourn his death. He was my father. You attribute far too much importance to the mere fact of having been to bed with another man, or with other men."

The delicately manicured and expensively ringed hand of the mother flashed against the son's cheek. The boy turned his back on her and stared intently at the rows of books, as though they held some deep interest for him. He was in tears.

The Chief Superintendent interrupted. "This is none of our business. I want to know from you, Signora, if you have grounds for suspicion regarding the murder of your husband."

She shrugged her shoulders. "He was Sicilian," she said, "and the Sicilians have been killing each other for years. You tell me why."

"What insight!" said the son ironically, returning to his seat on the other side of the desk from the Chief Superintendent.

"What about you? What's your opinion? What do you know?" the Chief Superintendent asked him.

"As to why he was killed, nothing. I was hoping to find out from you, sooner or later ... For the rest ..." He told them about his father's decision to return and unearth the Garibaldi and Pirandello letters, of his own regret at not being able to accompany him, or the telephone call assuring him that the journey had gone well. Nothing else.

"Tell me something about your properties here. Were they completely abandoned?"

"Yes and no. Every so often my father would write to someone or other, a priest, I think, to ask about the general state of maintenance."

"Had the priest been put in charge of the upkeep?"

"Not exactly, as far as I know."

"Did your father send him any money?"

"I don't think so."

"Did he reply to your father's letters?"

"Yes, he always said that everything was in good order, even though no one was living there."

"Did this priest have the keys of both the town house and the villa?"

"I don't know."

"Do you remember his name?"

"Cricco, I think ... Father Cricco ... But I couldn't be sure."

TEN

Father Cricco – a striking man, tall and stern in his clerical attire – insisted that he had never had the keys in his possession. At the most, he had peered into the town house and the country villa from the outside, and his reports were limited to issuing assurances that they were still standing, without prominent cracks or irreparable damage.

The Inspector, all deference and finely turned compliments, conducted the interrogation, while the sergeant wrote out what was said. The first words were: "You are one of the few priests who still dress as priests, and I personally find this greatly cheering, even if I am at a loss to explain why."

"I am an old-fashioned priest, and you are an old-fashioned Catholic. And both of us are much the better for it, if I may say so."

"As a priest, as an intelligent man, as a friend of the dead man, what is your opinion of this case?"

"In spite of the elaborate fiction which is being constructed around this business, I have to confess that I cannot get the likelihood of suicide out of my mind. Giorgio did not have peace of heart."

"Indeed: that wife of his, that son who was not his son . . ."

"I understand that the police scientific unit . . ."

"That's right, they found more than one fingerprint belonging to the deceased on the gun, but at the very point where his hand should have gripped it most tightly if he was to shoot himself, the prints seemed to have been rubbed out, as though the gun had been held by a gloved hand . . . but I, with the greatest respect for the scientific unit, have little faith in this finding."

The sergeant, who could not rid himself of the vice of butting in, said: "I have practically no faith in them either, but it is hard to imagine a man getting out a gun and then, on the very point of committing suicide, putting on a glove, shooting himself and still leaving himself the time to take the glove off and tidy it away. Quite a vaudeville turn, eh?"

"Enjoying ourselves, are we? You carry on enjoying yourself," said the Inspector, sourly.

ELEVEN

The police and judicial authorities decided that a further search of the villa was necessary, and decreed that the presence of mother and son, as well as of Professor Franzo, was indispensable. The Inspector, the sergeant and a group of policemen went along. Father Cricco declined the invitation: he was a highly emotional man, and in any case his presence would serve no purpose.

The sergeant was dispatched to collect the Professor from his house. They made the brief journey on their own, to the great delight of the sergeant who was always intoxicated by the prospect of talk with people who enjoyed a reputation for intelligence and culture. In the event, the professor spoke exclusively of his aches and pains, producing a phrase which the sergeant savoured but, in the full energy of his thirty years, could not accept, to the effect that at a certain point in life, instead of hope being the last to die, dying is the last hope.

The professor knew the place well, having spent many hours of his childhood and youth there in the company of his friend. As soon as he was inside the compound he pointed to the barns and said: "They were once the stables". The sergeant was taken aback to discover that the doors were wide open and that the chains had been removed. He assumed it must have been the Carabinieri and mentioned as much to the Inspector. Later, once they had returned home, they phoned the Carabinieri, but they knew nothing about the matter.

Nervously, the sergeant examined the barns one by one. A smell of something indefinable, perhaps burnt sugar, soaked eucalyptus leaves or alcohol, hung in the air. He said to the Inspector: "Do you smell that?"

"Smell what?"

"Isn't there a strange smell in the air?"

"I can't smell a thing. I've got a bit of a cold."

"We should get some expert, a chemist or something, to come along; maybe we'd be better with those dogs the Customs use."

"There's no dog like you, from the Customs or elsewhere," said the Inspector. "However, just to keep you happy, we'll bring in the boffins and the dogs."

The others were waiting in front of the door of the villa. The Inspector handed the keys to the sergeant saying: "You open up and guide us round. I've never been here before."

They all swarmed in, the officers in a frenzy of excitement, as though expecting to catch a burglar red-handed, the boy gazing around with eyes glistening with emotion and the woman ice-cold, as though bored.

On the ground floor there was nothing new for the officers, nothing they had not seen before. They made their way up to the first floor and trooped into the kitchen. The trap-door which led to the attic was lying open, revealing only darkness. They all stopped, until the Inspector pushed forward and climbed nimbly and sure-footedly up the wooden ladder. When he reached the top, the attic and the people at the foot of the steps were suddenly flooded in a bright light.

The sergeant, moving gingerly among the various objects piled pell-mell on the floor, scrutinized the walls with evident care.

"What are you looking for?" asked the Inspector.

"The switch."

"Of course, you never managed to locate it. There's no problem. It's here, behind the bust of St Ignatius."

"But you can't see it," said the sergeant.

"Intuition," said the Inspector. He risked a joke: "You're

not going to tell me I found it because I've been to University?" His eyes, however, glazed over, as though in terror.

"I didn't say a word," said the sergeant, darkly.

TWELVE

On the chest there was an outline mark, not covered by the same thick layer of dust which had settled everywhere else, which indicated that something had lain there for a considerable period. The rolled-up canvas, thought the sergeant, and said so. Poor Roccella had obviously seen it even before opening the chest to look for the letters. They were inside in two neat bundles, one containing those from Pirandello and the other those from Garibaldi. The professor had even seen them, years previously. He turned the pages of Pirandello's correspondence, pausing over the occasional arresting phrase. At eighteen, Pirandello was already thinking the thoughts that would still appear in his writing when he was well into his sixties.

On the return journey, the professor said to the sergeant: "I would be glad of the chance to read those letters of Pirandello's at greater leisure."

"There should be no problem in getting hold of them," said the sergeant, but his mind was elsewhere, and his mood was dark, unsettled, edgy. He felt the need to confide in someone, to give vent to his worries. Along the road, he stopped the engine and broke into hysterical tears. "We've been together for three years, in the same office."

"I understand," said the professor. "The light switch."

"The light switch ... he said he had never been in that house before. You heard him yourself. I went through a whole box of matches searching for that switch; the rest of them spent ages groping about the room with their torches looking for it, and yet he found it right away, first time."

"An unbelievable mistake on his part," said the professor.

"How could he have done it, what happened to him at that moment?"

"Perhaps the phenomenon of instant personality split: at that very moment he became the policeman hunting for himself." Enigmatically, as though talking to himself, he added: "Pirandello."

"I want to tell you about every single thing, starting from the light switch. I am putting it all together with mathematical precision."

"Mathematical," smiled the professor. "But there is always some lurking doubt."

"That's why I'm asking your help."

"What little I can do ... why not come up to my house. We'll get more peace."

They talked for hours, coming to the conclusion that, as far as the gang was concerned, the canvas was an ill-advised venture, a marginal activity, almost a piece of whimsy. The place was being used for purposes of a quite different order, and that was why the unfortunate Roccella, turning up unexpectedly, had to be murdered.

As they stood at the door saying good-night, the professor asked:

"Do you intend ..."

"I really don't know, answered the sergeant, unnerved and distraught, "I just do not know."

THIRTEEN

The following morning the Inspector arrived at the office at the usual time, in his customary high, almost euphoric, spirits. He removed his hat, his gloves, his overcoat, his bright but elegant scarf; he stuck the gloves in the pockets of his coat and hung them all in his personal cupboard. The gloves. While the Inspector, as every other morning, was trembling with the cold, saying that the birds would fall dead from the sky, the sergeant was already behind his desk, trembling for a different reason. The gloves, of course, the gloves.

"Hard at work already," said the Inspector, by way of greeting.

"It's hardly work. I'm just reading the morning papers."

"Anything interesting?"

"Interesting? No, no more than usual."

Behind that exchange of banal and unremarkable pleasantries there lay an unease, a coldness, a feeling of fear and concern.

The switch. The gloves. The sergeant neither knew, nor would have appreciated, a famous series of engravings by Max Klinger with the appropriate title *A Glove*, but in his mind the Inspector's glove flew, soared and puffed itself out as it had once done in the imagination of Max Klinger.

Their desks were at right-angles to each other. Each was seated at his own desk, the Inspector pretending to be immersed in the documents in front of him, the sergeant in the perusal of the newspapers.

Several times the sergeant was on the point of rising to his feet and going to the Chief Superintendent to report the whole story, but he was held back by the thought that the Chief Superintendent would regard all he had to say as lacking substance. The Inspector – as the sergeant immediately noticed – had other and more directly murderous thoughts on his mind.

After a certain time, the Inspector got up and went over to a little cupboard, took out a bottle of lubricating oil, a woollen duster and a pipe-cleaner. He said: "It must be years since I gave this gun a good cleaning."

He removed it from the holster on his belt, placed it carefully on the table, opened the barrel and let the bullets fall on to the table top.

The sergeant understood immediately. On the newspaper which he held open in front of his face, and which he continued to pretend to read, the sergeant saw the words dissolve, melt and merge into one huge headline which he believed he could read on the following day's front page:

POLICE INSPECTOR KILLS JUNIOR OFFICER
IN TRAGIC ACCIDENT.

He said: "I always clean my own . . . are you a good shot?"

"Excellent," said the Inspector.

The sergeant, to give due warning and keep faith with his own conscience, went on: "Look, to be a good shot, it's not enough to score a bull's eye . . . You need swiftness of hand, skill . . ."

"I know."

No you don't, thought the sergeant, you don't know at all. Or at least, you don't know in the way I do.

Every morning, he meticulously placed his own pistol in the top right-hand drawer of the desk, and now he leaned over and opened it slowly, quietly with his right hand, while with the left he kept the paper upright in front of him. His fingers had suddenly acquired a greater nimbleness, his hands seemed in some way to have multiplied, and each of his senses was keenly alert. Every part of his being quivered like a fine, tightly drawn cord, while the atavistic instinct of the peasant to be distrustful, suspicious, vigilant, to expect the worst and not be surprised by it when it came, had been reawakened in him to the point of paroxysm.

The Inspector finished cleaning his pistol, reloaded it, gripped it firmly in his hand, taking mock aim at the calendar, the light bulb, the door handle, but at the moment when, with unexpected speed, he swung round, pointed it at the sergeant and fired, the sergeant had already thrown himself and his chair to the ground, had pulled from behind the newspaper in his left hand the pistol he had removed from the drawer, had fired a shot at the Inspector's heart, and was watching him crumple on top of the papers spread in front of him, staining them with blood.

"He was a good shot," said the sergeant, gazing at the bullet-hole on the wall behind his desk, "but I did warn him." He sounded for a moment as though he had won a prize, but immediately afterwards he burst into tears and his teeth began chattering uncontrollably.

FOURTEEN

"Where have we got to?" said the Chief Superintendent. "Can we recapitulate and decide what we're doing . . . I mean, recapitulate and let the Procurator decide what he's doing. The journalists will be banging at the door in no time."

They were in the Procurator's office. The Carabinieri Colonel was there too, with the brigadier standing in front of them like an accused in the High Court dock.

"Where are we then . . . According to the sergeant's account, and an account, I may say, not without collaborative detail and elements to which, I am obliged to admit, I failed to attach due weight, according to his account the material facts are those which I will now briefly set out. On the evening of the eighteenth, a telephone call from Signor Roccella was logged in the police station. He requested someone to go to his house in order to see a certain object. The sergeant replied that someone would go at the earliest opportunity. He then communicated the content of the call to the Inspector, offering to go himself. The Inspector claims not to believe in the return of Signor Roccella after so many years. He considers the matter a hoax. He tells the sergeant to drop by at the locus the following morning, and goes off, having announced that for the whole of the following day, being the feast of St Joseph, he will be out of circulation, as indeed proved to be the case. It takes no great effort to suspect that he used the time to alert his accomplices of the unforeseen return of Signor Roccella, and takes even less effort to suspect that he went there in person, had himself admitted in his capacity as Police Inspector, sat at Roccella's side at the desk where the latter had begun to write about the canvas he had just found, and then, at the right moment, since the pistol on the desk-top presented an unhoped for opportunity, took the gun in his gloved hand and shot Roccella in the head. He then added a full stop after the 'I have found', and, having closed the door, which had a spring-lock, behind him, he went out ... I have to say, in self-criticism, that the full stop after the 'I have found', which the sergeant indicated to me as incongruous, did not at the time make any impact on me. I regarded Roccella as on the verge of insanity, and believed that he had come to see suicide as the solution. I further believed that he passionately desired to kill himself under the very eyes of the police ... However, the following day the body would unfailingly have been discovered. Hence the need for the speedy evacuation. At dead of night, the whole gang was summoned to the spot. The painting and other implements of clandestine work were transported elsewhere."

"Where?" asked the magistrate.

"In the opinion of the sergeant, which I fully share, to the Monterosso station. The station-master and assistant were members of the gang, even if fringe members, involved in distribution or drug pushing ... Doubtless, on seeing that quantity of compromising material being delivered, the pair of them took fright. They must have made protests, threats. As a result they were killed. They were already dead when the Volvo man made his appearance at the station. This explains the sudden flight ... The Volvo man did not see the station-master and assistant; he saw their killers ... this has been established by showing him the photographs of the station-master and assistant: he denied having seen them. Subsequently there was the episode of the light switch, which made a deep impression, and not only, I may say, on the sergeant."

"What an idiot!" said the magistrate. It was the only panegyric the Inspector would receive. He went on: "On the other hand, my dear Colonel, my dear Chief Superintendent, this is not quite enough ... suppose we were to reverse the whole story and consider that the sergeant might be lying. What if he were responsible for the deeds of which he is now accusing the Inspector?"

Chief Superintendent and Colonel exchanged those knowing looks which expressed the "Good God!" and the "Quite terrifying!" which a few days previously they had been able to exchange in words.

"It is out of the question," they both said at the same time. The Chief Superintendent invited the sergeant to step outside a moment: "Go into the waiting-room. We'll call you back in five minutes."

It was more than an hour before they called him back.

"An accident," said the magistrate.

"An accident," said the Chief Superintendent.

"An accident," said the Colonel.

And the following day, in the morning papers:

FATAL ACCIDENT
— SERGEANT CLEANING GUN SHOOTS INSPECTOR

FIFTEEN

While they were preparing the room in the police station to lay out the Inspector's body – it had been decided to bury him with full honours – the Volvo man was released from prison. He was brought to the station to go through the bureaucratic procedures which would grant him, finally, his liberty.

Having completed the formalities, he was making his way out of the station, flushed and nervously giggling, when he ran into Father Cricco, resplendent in surplus, biretta and stole, arriving to perform the last rites on the corpse.

Father Cricco stopped him with a gesture. He said: "Don't I know you? Aren't you one of my parishioners?"

"Parishioner! Me! I don't belong to anyone's parish," said the man, and went on his way deliriously happy.

He discovered a parking-ticket on the windscreen of his Volvo, but such was his state of mind, he merely laughed it off.

He was singing as he left the city, but all of a sudden he drew up sharply. His mood grew darker, his anxiety returned in full force. "That priest," he said to himself, "that priest . . . I would have recognised him immediately if it hadn't been for the clerical garb. That was the station-master, or at least the one I took for the station-master."

For a moment he was about the turn back to the police-station, but changed his mind on the instant. "What are you thinking about? Going back there to get yourself into an even bigger mess?"

He continued on his journey home, singing at the top of his voice.

Open Doors

TRANSLATED BY MARIE EVANS

The fact is, it is not the legislator who kills, but the judge, not the legislative ruling, but the judicial ruling. Thus the trial stands with total autonomy before the law and its injunctions, an autonomy in which and through which the injunction, as an arbitrary act of authority, melts away, and the trial, imposing itself on both the object and the originator of the injunction, and without any revolutionary implication, finds its "moment of eternity".

SALVATORE SATTA,
Soliloqui e colloqui di un giurista.

Preface

1937 might be seen, with hindsight, as a point of suspension in Mussolini's Italy, when the temporary euphoria inspired by the seizure of Abyssinia in spring 1936 was giving way to unease about Mussolini's other major initiatives of the same year: his prompt and lavish support in war materials and troops for Franco's attack on the Spanish republic, and his instigation of the Rome-Berlin Axis, which would soon lead to the subservience of Italy to Nazi Germany. These events were seen by many as the beginning of a universal conflict between Fascism and democracy. After 1938, Mussolini's popularity would go into an irreversible decline.

But in 1937 he had been in power for fifteen years, and a total dictator for more than a decade. Corporatism, perhaps the only theory that an opportunist movement might be said to have elevated to the status of a political philosophy, was established in 1926 by the Rocco Law, named after the Minister of Justice, independent trade unions having previously been outlawed. However valuable the theory of corporations of employees and employers, in practice it was merely part of the power structure, providing jobs for the party faithful and abundant opportunity for corruption and for labour exploitation. Unemployment was always high – possibly as high as two million in 1932; real wages fell by about 11% between 1925 and 1938, and there was a decline in standard of basic foods and general health among workers.

Total obedience was demanded from Italians of all ages. Membership of the various Fascist youth movements, starting with the Balilla at the age of four, became compulsory. Out of 1200 professors, only 11 refused the loyalty oath and they were forced into retirement. Standard punishment for political offenders was "confino", sometimes on a penal island, but often to a remote mainland district under surveillance, where life could be extremely primitive. Culture and intellectual pursuits were scorned, except as a means of glorifying fascism under the aegis of the Fascist Institute of Culture and the School of Fascist Mysticism. Mussolini was a powerful journalist and demagogue, and poured money into his propaganda machine. Press censorship was imposed early and Fascists put in charge of the well-known liberal papers.

Mussolini's was not a murderous regime compared with Hitler's or Stalin's, but violence was rife in the early years, abating after 1925, partly for lack of opposition, since most dissenters had either been variously silenced or chosen to leave the country. One murder in 1924 caused such revulsion that it rocked Mussolini's power. A Socialist deputy, Giacomo Matteotti, protested eloquently in the Chamber of Deputies against the Fascist terror tactics in the April elections; on 10 June he was attacked by five men and taken off in a car; in August his body was found in a shallow grave with multiple stab wounds. By the end of the year Mussolini's "consuls'- compelled him to reassert himself by a return to force. A secret police force was created in 1926, whose arbitrary procedures included torture, together with Special Tribunals for the Defence of the State. The death penalty, which had been abandoned in Italy forty years earlier, was reintroduced, and became identified with Fascism and its boasted law and order.

It is within this system of fear and oppression that Sciascia's "little judge" conducts this murder trial in Palermo in 1937.

Marie Evans

NOTE: ★ in the text refers to an entry in the brief notes on pp. 201–2

ONE

"You know my thinking," said the District Prosecutor. The perfect opening for the man whose thinking you don't know, or if he has "a thinking", or if he thinks at all. The little judge looked at him gently, sleepily, a lingering, indulgent look. And the prosecutor felt the look on his face, just as once, as a boy, he had felt the hand of an old, blind relative who wanted – he said – to see which of the older members of the family he resembled. The hand of that relative whom he'd never met before, moving over his face as though modelling it, had aroused in him a certain repugnance, disgust. And now this look caused him irritation and anxiety. Who was the little judge likening him to? And he regretted the sentence which had been meant to open a confiding, almost friendly discussion. But he could think of nothing better than to turn it round. He said: "I know your thinking." But still that look, increasing his irritation and anxiety. He skipped the whole argument he had carefully prepared and as if grasping at air said: "It must be admitted they have never asked anything of us. Even in this case – let's be quite clear about this – they have made no demands."

The Prosecutor's imposing stature, and the imposing chair he usually sat in, made the little judge uneasy and embarrassed, and in their rare conversations this unease always turned to indifference and boredom: his mind wandered, or gave an ironic twist to the phrases it caught. "His thinking, my thinking: what a silly, tedious game. I don't know his thinking and I don't want to know; but I don't have a "thinking" at all: I just think." And his mind dwelt on the phrase whose essence no grammar or dictionary would register as a substitute for the thing you don't want to name, the thing you don't want to think: especially when the possessive pronoun precedes the thinking, and nothing follows. A phrase that, for Italians, belonged to the Catholic religion, the governing party, freemasonry, anything that had – obviously, or worse, obscurely – force and power, anything to be feared; and now belonged to Fascism, its rulings and its rituals. "You know my thinking, I know your thinking: so let's not think about it. That's the best thing."

Like a landscape out of the mist, the Prosecutor's words floated to the surface of his mind. He was saying: "They set up their special tribunals, they kept us outside and – why shouldn't we say it – above politics, their politics: and we still have judges, functioning without any interference, who have not only passed sentences that were unpopular with some official or even with the regime, but have quite openly and firmly ignored the pronouncement of some official or some group or of the entire party, on certain cases or certain interpretations of the laws . . ."

"Yes, outside or above: but their special tribunals . . ."

"We couldn't oppose them: we would have lost what we have managed to hold on to."

"We went along with it."

"Yes, we went along with it," the Prosecutor admitted. A sigh of resignation turned into a yawn. He yawned frequently: because of something going on in his body that he chose to ignore; but also because of the life he led, caught between the huge power his office gave him, which he exercised with obsessive caution and concern, and that which his family, caring only for his salary, utterly denied him. "But you know my thinking," he said again. And again he yawned, this time for the tedium of having to work out his thinking, if only on a matter of detail, losing sight, as always, of the whole. But all at once he lost sight of that detail too, descending to another, more concrete. He opened a desk drawer and pulled out a red folder. He held it between his hands to surprise the judge at the right moment. "The police", he said, "sent us all the papers found in the defendant's house. All except this one. It was included in the list that accompanied the others, but was held back at the police station. I had to insist to get hold of it. Why, I said, and wrote, why send us so many papers, even useless ones – agendas, letters, postcards, family photos, butcher's bills, baker's bills – and not this one? It seems they had orders from above not to give it to us. If I ask myself why, one answer does occur to me: but perhaps it's not the right one. So I'd like to hear your opinion – yesterday, at last, they gave way." And he gave way, holding the folder out to the judge.

The judge took it, and as he glanced at it he gave a start: it was an image which, thirteen years before, newspapers, manifestos, even postcards had as it were hammered into the memory of Italians with a memory, into the feelings of Italians with feelings. This very image: a serene, severe countenance, broad brow, thoughtful gaze with something sorrowful, even tragic about it; or perhaps with the tragic touch conferred upon his living image by his tragic death. An image which took the judge back to that summer of 1924 (he was a *pretore* in a little country district in Sicily where there were few Fascists and fewer Socialists) when the fate of Fascism seemed to hang in the balance, but as the summer waned, to reassert itself and get the upper hand. And in his memory the sense, literally the sense – colours, smells, even tastes – of the dying summer was associated with the waning of the passions that tragic case had kindled even in ordinary homes. A passion he too had felt, but within a passion for law, justice and right. And he thought: "A feeling like that was never meant to die."

Beside the photo, spattered with dots and exclamation marks, was the passage in which were phrases attributed to Giacomo Matteotti, addressed "to his executioners" like these: "kill me, but you will never kill the idea that is in me; my ideas cannot die; my little ones will glory in their father; the workers will bless my corpse; long live Socialism." And from these ingenuously solemn and heroic phrases (which nonetheless, he remembered, proved effective not only in encouraging the opposition but in moving the hearts of housewives), the word "corpse" stood out starkly, and the image in front of him dissolved into another: the photograph showing the "mortal remains" being carried from the Quartarella woods to the cemetery at Riano Flaminio: the whitewood box, the four carabinieri carrying it: and the first one (on the left in the photo, he recalled with terrible precision), closest to the camera, holding a handkerchief to his nose and mouth. For years now, whenever certain facts at certain moments had reminded him of the murder of Matteotti, he had thought of it only in words belonging to subsequent history and its verdict; but this red folder had thrown him right back into visual memories whose clarity and precision surprised him, but which were steeped in those words and that verdict. Photographs from the weekly magazine that printed more than any other at the time: the women of Riano carrying flowers to the place where the body had been found; the funeral at Fratta Polesine, the coffin carried on the shoulders of relatives and friends (the baritone Titta Ruffo, a cousin, was singled out in the caption: had he paid dearly for that relationship and that devotion?); and the most remarkable image of all, that said more than a whole chapter in a history book, of those Socialist deputies kneeling near the parapet of the bridge where Matteotti had been seized. They had laid a wreath and knelt down: eyes eager to pass into history turned towards the camera; some at the back had got to their feet, fearing the lens would miss them. And he thought he would look out the photograph: he remembered two or three names of the kneeling men, and was curious to know what had become of them all.

One thought led to another, and he found himself saying

rashly: "One thing nobody paid much attention to at the time: he was a qualified teacher of criminal law at the university of Bologna."

"Who?" asked the Prosecutor.

"Matteotti," said the judge: but the Prosecutor's guarded, almost pitying look suggested not only wariness, but a suspicion of muddled thinking, of talking in non sequiturs, what had the detail of being a qualified teacher to do with such a thorny subject? But that detail had told the judge something: that Matteotti had been considered the most implacable of all the opponents of Fascism, not because he spoke in the name of Socialism, which was then an open door that anyone could pass through, but because he spoke in the name of the law. Of criminal law.

The Prosecutor gave him time to switch back to the topic he had invited him there to discuss; then he asked with a yawn: "What do you think? I mean, about the fact that they didn't want to send us this particular document."

"Delicacy," said the judge.

"Quite so," said the Prosecutor, irritated as he always was when he suspected sarcasm or irony. "It seems to me that, in drawing attention to the omission, and persisting in it, they were telling us: we don't want to confuse the issue and accuse the defendant of a crime of a quite different order, although it might be necessary to bear it in mind as a detail which completes the whole wretched picture; besides, you have plenty of evidence on which to base the harshest verdict."

"Indelicacy, then," commented the judge.

"Never mind delicacy and indelicacy, let's take it for what it is: a warning ... The fact is, they expect a swift exemplary sentence."

There was a knock, the Prosecutor said: "Come in"; the usher came in with a bundle of post and put it on the table. As soon as he had gone out again, shutting the door behind him, the Prosecutor said: "A spy: I suspect a high-ranking one, and well paid; I got the carabinieri to enquire very discreetly: he lives way above his salary. Or mine ... At this moment he'll certainly have his ear glued to the door. But only for art's sake: you can't hear anything, I've checked."

The judge longed to cut short this conversation, in which he felt uneasily he must either reveal his true feelings or lie. Or worse still: fail both to conceal his feelings and to lie. He tried a short cut: "So you say they expect a swift, exemplary sentence. But they're not the only ones: I am well aware that everyone expects it."

The Prosecutor looked relieved. "Let's speak quite clearly about it then," he said: but instead he fell silent for some time, as if waiting for a slow-dawning light to clarify what he had to say. At last, like a hunting-dog returning from some distant trail: "The prosecuting service and the judiciary: it's almost a commonplace to believe that the judiciary, to which you belong, has nothing to do with political power and has remained absolutely independent these last years; while people think quite the opposite about the prosecuting service ... But I could quote as many cases of submission on both sides. Cases, I may say, which cannot be assumed to prove real dependency on either side. But let's admit the truth of the commonplace, and that you too, at this very moment, believe it to be true and see in my words some sort of message, an oblique threat, that the political powers have charged me to convey ... It's not true; but go ahead and think it, if you like ..."

The judge moved his right hand in a gesture of denial: the gesture of a boy wiping something off a blackboard. And he really did not believe it: the Prosecutor was not a bad fellow; almost always boring, but never underhand; outside the corporate body arrogant at times, but within the confraternity capable of only small, fairly harmless deceptions.

"If you don't believe it at this moment," the Prosecutor went on, with his inveterate pessimism, "you'll end up believing it tomorrow or next year ... Anyway, the point is this: I remember, about ten years ago, a discussion we had about the death penalty. We were not alone, if you recall. An article by His Excellency Rocco had just come out, in the review *The Empire* ... Here it is: I read it through again this morning ..." He pulled the review out from under the bundle of letters, and opened it at a marker. "Here it is: *On the re-introduction of the death penalty in Italy* ... I don't remember the arguments you used to refute it, but I remember your tone of extreme irritation. And I grant you, his introduction is rather irritating: "*The return*," he read, "*of the death penalty in Italy demanded by the national conscience, invoked by the Chamber of Deputies, decided by His Majesty's Government satisfies an ancient wish of Italian wisdom*: which is a bit much, I admit ... But I was and am entirely in agreement with the arguments developed in the article." He waited for the judge to say something. Disappointed, he went on: "Believe it or not, out of the respect I feel for you and, if you will permit me to say so, out of a feeling of good will, of friendship ..."

"Thank you," said the judge.

"... I merely ask you to think twice about this trial which is due to come up in your Court: and above all, if it poses problems for you, assuming your opinions on the death penalty are unchanged, to turn it down or – it's not my field – get together with the President of the Court of Appeal to find the most convenient, least prejudicial way of transferring it to another session ... Least prejudicial, I mean, to your career: a brilliant one up to now, it seems to me ... I said it before and I say it again, I am entirely in agreement with the theses of His Excellency Rocco," he never forgot to give the title he boasted to anyone else with a claim to it, "and therefore in agreement with the law, since the death penalty has been a State law for ten years now: law is law, we can only apply it and serve it. And this, of all cases, would seem to call for capital punishment, since capital punishment is now the law of the land; these are cold, brutal crimes; the man is the lowest of the low ... The whole town is up in arms, appalled: in a lynching mood ... But I seem to recall – I say it without irony, indeed with regret, almost with pain – that you would prefer lynching –"

"I would not prefer it. I said at the time, I recall, that a band of fanatics or drunks who think they are making their own justice, in fact corroborate the law by contravening it: in the sense that the action imposes on its agents the indemnification of the law, an affirmation that must not, can not be ... But surely the instincts that erupt in a lynching, the fury and madness, are less atrocious than the macabre ritual that activates a court of justice in pronouncing the death sentence: a sentence which, in the very name of justice, law, reason, of the King, by the grace of God and the will of the nation, consigns a man, the way it is done here, to be shot by twelve rifles; twelve rifles aimed by twelve men who were enlisted for the good of the people, the ultimate good which is life, but who at a particular moment in time have responded eagerly to a call to commit murder, not only unpunished but rewarded ... A vocation to murder fulfilled with the State's gratitude and remuneration."

"Let's not exaggerate," said the Prosecutor. He was quite thrown; the "at the time" with which the judge had begun, distancing into memory the opinion he had held ten years before, had led him to expect a different, changed opinion now; but the ensuing vehemence accorded ill with the "at the time".

Generally a taciturn man of few and well-honed words, the little judge seemed a prey to uncontrollable eloquence. "Do you know," he went on, "how a firing squad is formed? I don't mean by the military and in time of war, when there's an obligation to take part: I mean here and now, in peacetime, in the system we administer ... Have you ever seen the men in a squad? Black uniforms; black capes when I saw them; faces that lend conviction to Lombroso's theories on the physiognomy of criminals, faces that in a barracks of the guardia or the carabinieri, where they are performing the duties for which they were enrolled, we might say showed

136

atavistic deprivation and brutality: but looking at them, and knowing that these are the faces of men who have chosen to kill, who have been chosen to kill ... They call them 'metropolitani', they arrive like a flock of crows, a flock of death, from the capital: a curious association of the capital city with capital punishment."

"Never mind that," said the prosecutor, irritated by the judge's emotion and a little by his own. And he thought: "I wash my hands of it"; and thought it so intensely that he made the gesture. "Never mind that ... But whatever your thinking, and whatever my thinking on the matter, we must consider ..." That phrase again: but this time it was a technical, a "shop" matter, a more or less pointless debating matter within a confraternity, since the law was stronger than any opinion: "... we must consider that no novelistic fancy could confer the slightest doubt or the slightest ambiguity on this case, not the faintest echo of pity or mercy: unless for the victims, of course; nor project it in such a way as to arouse regret for the old State or criticism of the new. Impossible to turn it into anything like the Sergeant Grischa question, believe me." Arnold Zweig's novel had been on the Prosecutor's latest reading list*: it wasn't really relevant, but the Prosecutor was keen to show himself a man of literary pursuits, and besides he wanted to change the subject slightly. And indeed, the judge asked: "What question is that?"

"I don't know what historical or documentary basis it has. A novel. By a German. Very interesting: the old Prussian state with its princes, its rules, its scruples, losing out in the clash against post-war Germany and its petty tyrannies, disregard for law, total lack of scruple, its inhuman abstraction ... The Germany of today: and let's hope ours will stop in time, that they won't get us too compromised in that liaison ..." But he realised he was getting too compromised himself, and "Let's get back to the point ... You know it's generally felt here that since Fascism you can sleep with open doors ..."

"I always close mine," said the judge.

"So do I: but we must admit that for the past fifteen years conditions of public safety have improved considerably. Even in Sicily, in spite of everything. Now, whatever we think about the death penalty, we must admit that its reintroduction serves to hammer home the idea of a State totally dedicated to the safety of its citizens; the idea that from now on people really can sleep with open doors."

"I wouldn't deny it," said the judge.

"So we agree," said the Prosecutor, with the haste of a man afraid to find they don't agree in the least. He got up, the judge got up, they shook hands. "May I ask you," said the judge, "to lend me this review? I should like to re-read the article by His Excellency Rocco." The Prosecutor gave it to him, led him to the door, opened it: the usher was standing outside, a false obsequiousness making his real expression even more disagreeable: greedy and ferrety. Looking at him, Prosecutor and judge remembered they had doubly infringed the Fascist party code: they had used the formal "you" to each other and shaken hands. They took leave using "voi" and giving the Fascist salute.

The Prosecutor went back into his office and returned to his lofty chair. He yawned wearily. "Whatever his thinking, he will have to reflect, weigh the pros and cons ... After all, it's his career!" But we are often wrong to judge our fellows as our fellows in every way. Some are worse, but some are better, too.

TWO

The conversation with the Prosecutor had lasted a very long time (much longer than it will have seemed to the reader). When the judge left the Palace of Justice it was already evening, street-lamps were already lit, the great trees on the square formed dark masses, their branches monstrously articulated. Every time he crossed the threshold of this palace, the word "inquisition" flashed through the judge's mind. For a couple of centuries it was here that blasphemers, witches, heretics, often of no known heresy, were judged; from this portico the *auto da fé* processions had wound through the town to the fire that would be lit not far away, though the plan of the route and the slowness of the cortège made it seem very far indeed. The State – the Bourbon State, the State of Savoy – was obviously fated, given the shortage of public buildings, to inherit this palace from the Inquisition; but it was by a choice made law that it had also inherited the conduct of fiscal proceedings against the heretics, appropriating the estates of the condemned and disputing interminably with the legitimate heirs. One dispute had lasted until about 1910, over the estate of a Quietist heretic – a woman – (but the transgression had been sexual rather than doctrinal), who had been burnt in 1724. Money has no smell, not even of the living flesh burning at the stake which spectators at *auto da fé* maintain has a powerful and quite peculiar smell. "When all's said and done, it means attaching tremendous weight to one's own opinions if a man is roasted alive for their sake." Grand words; everything is a matter of opinion, of relative or derisory value, except the opinion that you can not roast a man alive because he does not share certain opinions. And except the opinion, here and now in 1937 (1987) that humanity, justice, law – in short, the State which the idealist philosophy and the doctrine of Fascism at the time called *ethical* – must not answer murder with murder.

Speaking of those years, perhaps of that very year, Vitaliano Brancati★ says of a poor man who felt a strong aversion to iniquity that he could find no words to explain: "Why did a canto on liberty by Milton or Leopardi, or a book by some outlawed philosopher not fly to the help of this poor man, suffering all the torment oppression can inflict upon an honest soul, yet incapable of explaining his suffering?" But the little judge was not lacking in such help. There were these indelible words: "When I saw how the head split away from the body, and how each landed separately in the crate, then I realised, not with my intelligence, but with my whole being, that there is no theory of the rationality of life or of progress that can justify such an act, and that even if everyone on earth since the world began, arguing from whatever theory, were to declare it necessary, I know that it is not necessary, that it is evil and therefore that neither the words and actions of men, nor progress itself can judge what is good and necessary, but only I, in my own heart." Words which, in our pursuit of the judge's thoughts, we failed to find in the translation he had acquired as a boy around Christmas 1913 (he remembered it exactly, because only at such a time, thanks to a gift from a relative in America, did he have the one and a half or two lire needed to buy it); so we have used another more recent one, knowing that no translation, neither the clumsiest nor the most beautiful (the most beautiful could be the most dangerous) will ever succeed in translating a great Russian writer. In the judge's mind too was another page by another Russian: "But the Prince was a half-wit – the lackey was quite sure of this . . .": that is, the Prince who is telling of an execution he has witnessed (again by the guillotine in Paris), and who pours out the most inspired attack on capital punishment that has ever been made. And the judge seemed to recall that the lackey had been moved at one point, but it could not have gone very deep, for lackeys are always in favour of capital punishment, those who are lackeys by their function and those who are lackeys in their soul.

Now here (he had arrived home, put on his slippers, opened the balcony windows, lit the lamp on his desk, and had begun to read the article *On the reintroduction of the death penalty in Italy*), here's this poor Rocco – and he really felt a sort of commiseration, almost pity for him – who starts with a long list of the great names of Italian and foreign "wisdom" who have approved, or even invoked, the death penalty. Wisdom, wisdom. Poor Rocco, Professor of Criminal Law in the Royal University of Rome, Minister of Justice (and Grace), His Excellency Rocco: titles perfectly suited to the garb of a lackey, but the title of Lawyer that he liked to put before his name, no, the judge really could not grant him that.

His Excellency Rocco: the Prosecutor was always referring to him. A good fellow, the Prosecutor, but good fellows form the base of every pyramid of iniquity. "In fact, I'm one of those good fellows, too." And even if the Prosecutor thought otherwise, the judge could not bring himself to believe, not even remotely, that the cautious admonition he had received was prompted by anything but a sense of corporate concern, by a hope of satisfying an almost universal demand for justice in this case, and perhaps by some personal esteem bordering on friendship, although there had never really been a proper friendship between them. According to his parents, his brothers and his wife, the judge's chief weakness was this: believing until direct evidence to the contrary, and even then viewing the evidence in an indulgent light, that there was more good than bad in everyone, and that in everyone the bad might suddenly prevail because of some absentmindedness, a false step, some fall of more or less vast and deadly consequence, both for oneself and others. A weakness that had prompted his calling to become a judge, and enabled him to carry out the task. Not that he did not feel touches of unkindness and spite, prickings of *amour propre*, but he sublimated them – at least he thought so and took comfort in the fact – in a sphere we might call literary and which he called innocent, in the sense that he considered they hurt no one. But we will use *literary*, giving it another, although not too serious sense, since literature is never wholly innocent. Not even the most innocent.

He had come to the end of Rocco's article: "As for cases involving the death penalty (whether this should be limited only to the gravest political crimes or only to the most brutal common crimes or extended to both and to those that lie between the two), likewise as to the mode of execution of the death penalty, and the judicial body to which it should be entrusted, the forms of procedure and judgement and so on, these are particular questions of criminal legislative policy which I consider must be left to the political wisdom of Government and Parliament. For they will know how to act in this as in other matters as sure and faithful interpreters of the juridical conscience of the Italian Nation." And "in this matter too" Rocco's expectations had not been disappointed. How could they be, since he was the prime contributor to their realisation?

He had failed to wax indignant in re-reading it, which had been his intention in asking the Prosecutor to lend it to him. Whereas the latter had thought he wanted to find in it reasons for rethinking his ideas, changing his mind. A good fellow, in favour of the death penalty as of something remote, willed by others, carried out by others, abstract, almost a propaganda show and, ultimately, aesthetic. He had never been required to call for it in a trial; and if it was called for by his substitutes, perhaps he thought it was their business, of no great weight since calling for it was quite different from carrying it out. And to give him his due, the judge thought, if he had been required to carry it out, at least the perception that it had been reintroduced to deceive the citizenry about improved law and order under the Fascist State, this dawning perception would have touched and troubled his conscience. Which would never have happened to Professor Rocco, who knew perfectly well the reason for the reintroduction.

He had failed to work up a fresh sense of indignation. As his chemistry master used to say, the solution was already saturated. Saturated with indignation.

THREE

Open doors. Supreme metaphor for order, security and trust: "You can sleep with the doors open." But in that sleep would be a dream of open doors, corresponding in everyday, wide-awake reality, especially for those who liked to stay awake and scrutinize and understand and judge, to so many closed doors. The newspapers, above all, were closed doors, but the citizens who spent thirty centesimi a day to buy one – two out of every thousand in the densely populated south – were unaware of this closed door, except when something happened before their own eyes, something serious or tragic, and they looked for news of it, and either did not find it or found it shamelessly impostured (the word is not considered good usage, we know, but we are sure the reader will forgive it if we offer in its justification the definitions that persuaded us to use it: "*Falsity* directly concerns things, insofar as they do not correspond to the concept in the mind; *falsehood* concerns words, insofar as they do not correspond to the heart; *imposture* concerns facts, insofar as words and actions and silence are directed to deceiving someone, that is, to make him believe untruths to the advantage of the deceiver, and to the satisfaction of some ignoble passion of his": definitions, I need hardly say, to be found in the great Tommaseo dictionary.)

In the case which was about to come before the judge – a man who had killed three people in a matter of hours – imposture had reached its apogee and toppled over into the grotesque or comic. The victims had been, in chronological order, the murderer's wife; the man who had taken over the murderer's job in the office from which he had been dismissed; and the man in charge of the office who had ordered his dismissal. But as far as the paper was concerned, there had been no murder: There was no mention of the wife, and the other two had died, albeit suddenly, a natural death. For two days reports had spoken of them, their sudden deaths, the funerals, the grief of the townspeople. So, as journalism moves onward and upward towards the magnificent destiny it must surely achieve, if it has not already done so, we thought it might serve as a model to offer the report as it appeared, the day after the tragic events, in the paper with the widest circulation in Sicily:

"The news of the sudden death of Avvocato Communale Giuseppe Bruno, President of the Fascist Provincial Union of Artists and Professionals and Secretary of the Legal Syndicate, has spread rapidly throughout our city, causing a general sense of profound grief in every area of life in which the deceased was so highly esteemed for his noble qualities of heart and mind.

"In Giuseppe Bruno, Palermo has lost one of its most active representatives, whose generous contribution to public life was always wide-ranging and invariably marked by balanced judgement, rectitude of feeling and nobility of intention.

"The outstanding qualities that so widely endeared him to all categories of artists and professional people in our city made him a distinguished syndicate chairman and administrative head. President of the Union of Artists and Professionals from its foundation, Secretary of the Legal Syndicate, Vice-Secretary of the Federation of Fascist Branches in Palermo, he was a wise organiser and promoter of every institution entrusted to his leadership.

"In the Palermo Law Courts in particular he will be remembered for his exquisite sense of justice, which made his presence a guarantee of harmony in every decision taken.

"In the administration of public affairs, as Municipal Assessor, Commissioner of the Water Board, Chairman of the Governing Body of the Hospital, member of the Governing Council of the Bank of Sicily, he displayed at all times the energy and passion with which he espoused the highest causes, born of a scrupulous and lofty sense of responsibility.

"The unfailing trust he earned among party leaders for his dignified conduct of the most delicate Fascist and Syndicalist functions in the province, was to him the cherished reward for his disinterested and devoted work as a party official.

"The grief of his afflicted family is therefore shared by the great family of artists and professional people in Palermo, by whom he will always be remembered as an example and a guide.

"Around his mortal remains today are dipped the banners of Fascism and of Syndicalism in Palermo, just as around his memory are gathered the grieving thoughts of all who knew him and were enabled to appreciate his noble qualities.

"The solemn honours which will be rendered to Giuseppe Bruno today will be a fitting testimony to these feelings.

"The body, lying in state at the Union of Artists and Professionals has been since yesterday evening the focus of a devoted pilgrimage on the part of the principal Fascist and Syndicalist leaders and officials, as well as a wide range of representatives from the various categories of artists and professional people.

"Conveyed late yesterday afternoon to the headquarters of the Union, the body has been the object of an all-night vigil by Young Fascists, and from nine in the morning all the representatives of the Union of Artists and Professionals will take turn in mounting guard until the cortège moves off.

"The funeral will be attended by the Party leaders and officials, and all the unions, led by the flag-bearers, secretaries and Presidents of the individual Directories.

"Party members will attend the funeral in Fascist uniform.

"Starting from Via Caltanissetta at 16 hours, the funeral cortège will proceed along the Vie Libertà, Ruggero Settimo,

Cavour and Via Roma. At the home of the deceased in Via
San Cristoforo, the hearse will pause for a few moments for
those present to pay homage to the birthplace of Giuseppe
Bruno. The cortège will disperse in piazza Giulio Cesare (at
the Central Station) with the Fascist salute.

"On receipt of these grim tidings, the Union of Artists and
Professionals wished to give immediate expression to their
profound grief, and arranged for General Officer Gennaro
Vitelli, President of the Union of Artists and Professionals in
Messina, to represent them.

"The ceremony in honour of the late-lamented Avv.
Comm. Giuseppe Bruno will be combined with the funeral of
Antonino Speciale, accountant to the Secretariat of the Legal
Syndicate, who yesterday was also suddenly taken from his
loving family and from all those in the legal world who so
highly valued his work.

"The body of Accountant Antonino Speciale is also lying in
a funeral chamber in the Union of Artists and Professionals,
watched over by Young Fascists and by the police."

The judge had placed this report, together with the next
day's describing the solemn "obsequies", in a file labelled
"non-existence of the crimes for which judgement upon the
man accused of them is entrusted to the second session of the
Assize Court of Palermo"; and he would have liked to take
the sad jest further, and insert the file among the documents of
the trial, fantasising about a possible, or impossible, incrimi-
nation of the paper and the reporter. To what legal "dictum",
properly or by analogy, could one resort to incriminate them?
Fantasies, to which the judge often succumbed, juridical day-
dreams in a scheme of things which, while leaving the letter
of the law intact, destroyed its substance.

In the report which we have extracted from this file there
was only one point you could call a wink and a nod from the
reporter to the reader, from the voluntary slave to the invo-
luntary slave: this was the word "grim", which, strictly in its
dictionary meaning, might be defended with the hierarchy

simply for its sense of grievous and doomed, undeniably, and pleonastically, every death is "grim"; but not one of its readers would have failed to reognise its sense of the dark, violent and bloody deed they were choosing to hide.

FOUR

When the trial began, in fact, at the very first session, in a flash of childish fancy born of the many fairy-tales that had marked his childhood, some funny, some frightening, the judge kept thinking what a good thing it would be to possess the power, some magic gift, to make the defendant invisible. To be precise, he did not think it: it was as if his thoughts were brushed, even suffused, for a moment by something vague and fleeting from a world of memory and dream, memory melting into dream. Sometimes it was only the flash of an object – a ring. Turn it round on the finger, and the man would vanish from the witness-box where he stood talking calmly with the two carabinieri at every pause in the proceedings. So that at times the judge was annoyed to catch himself twisting his wedding-ring on his finger.

The man made him terribly uneasy; almost as if, while unconsciously soliciting, and at times unbearably stimulating it, he prevented the dialogue with reason to which the judge was accustomed. And his instinct was to rub him out, as if from a drawing in which an allegorical representation of life – of the terrifying side of life, passions, violence, pain – became unbalanced by the excessive realism of this figure. An incongruous note. An error.

But the drawing from which to erase him and the magic ring to make him invisible were, as he knew to his great irritation, a transference, an alibi, an attempt to escape from the word and the judgement upon this man that the law expected of him. Therefore to yield to this instinct would be to take on the mantle of the Rocco doctrine, an acceptance that is total and unhesitating in those who demand the return of capital punishment, and when they have got it, want it to apply not only to murderers, but also to rapists, pickpockets and chicken-thieves, especially when they are the victims of the theft. But it could also be that those in favour of capital punishment were prompted by a sort of primordial, larval aesthetism. Aesthetic in two ways: because they wanted life cleansed and liberated from all extreme human degradation, that is, from those who have killed for degrading passions and degrading motives, and in degrading ways (deceit, betrayal), and must be considered unfit to live; and because, sometimes having witnessed it but usually in their imagination, they see the ordered ritual violence of this death-dealing, with its savage but considerate rules, as a pure spectacle, almost a fiction, assuming the death-dealers are concerned only to *perform it well*, and the recipient only to accept its inevitability and *behave well*. In short, what Stendhal called the sublime conceived by ignoble minds, when likening the torments depicted by Pomarancio and Tempesta in a church in Rome to the spectacle of the guillotine in action. And indeed, at every session, the judge felt an occasional stab of something ignoble, a contraction, pause, suspended animation as in a dream, the vertiginous horror and fascination of the void or abyss. It never lasted, but the uneasiness lingered. He had been allotted a case in which even the most just and serene of men, the most illuminated by what the theologians call Grace and laymen Reason, must come to terms with the darkest, most secret part of himself, in fact, the most ignoble.

And then, he was disturbed in a sort of gut reaction, a horror of the flesh rather than the mind, by the dagger, the "corpus delicti" lying on a corner of the table at which the clerk went on and on writing – never lifting his bald head, spectacles thick as bottle-glass – as if it were not he producing writing but the writing producing him like an excrescence. Placed on a sheet of newspaper – from his high seat the judge could read the banner headline: *The Duce to Franco on the first*

anniversary of his nomination as Head of the Spanish State –
the dagger, rusty with traces of blood, reminded him of the
defendant's words at the first interrogation, the one with the
police commissioner: "I had already envisaged the rash acts I
committed today, in that, at the time when I was no longer
receiving my salary, I bought fifty cartridges for the revolver
... I also bought a hunting knife ... and in the same period I
took a bayonet I had in the house to be sharpened by a knife-
sharpener in the Via Beati Paoli." (The right name, thought
the judge, for a street to get a dagger sharpened in, a weapon
of which that legendary sect made frequent and, according to
people of the same persuasion as the accused, perfectly justi-
fied use.) Determined to carry out the punishment he had
"envisaged" (all his experience with lawyers and magistrates
failed to alert him to the fact that he was confessing premeditation), he had collected the bayonet that morning, paying the
knife-sharpener one lira for sharpening it and shortening it to
the size of a dagger, and had put it into the belt of his trousers,
in the pocket of which he already had a pistol and twenty-five
cartridges. But he had chosen the dagger as the murder-
weapon; he said he meant to use the pistol to kill himself.

Why the dagger? Looking at it on the clerk's table, then
looking up as the defendant, the judge answered his own
question with a definition that was already in a book, but one
that he would never read, by a writer whose name he would
hear perhaps, but only his name, right at the end of his life:
"It is more than a simple metal object; men conceived and
forged it to a precise end; in a sense it is eternal: the dagger
that killed a man last night in Tacuarembó, or the daggers that
killed Caesar. It is meant to kill, to strike without warning, to
shed blood still pulsing." Exactly what the judge was thinking, but he extended the thought, opening it out into a fan of
sombre images and memories that were part of him, just as
suffering the consequences of a whole year of malaria was part
of him. The Arditi shock-troops arriving at the front for some
night sortie demanding silence and surprise, armed only with

daggers. The snipping of shears at barbed wire seemed to expand and echo like an alarm in the darkness of the night, and sometimes the alarm was really sounded in the enemy trench, so that the Arditi crawling towards it were met by a sudden burst of rifle and machine-gun fire. But the actions were usually successful, and when the Arditi returned and the infantry moved forward – a hundred, two hundred yards – to occupy the conquered enemy trench, there were the beardless Austrian soldiers stabbed in their sleep, or in their sudden, alarmed awakening. It was like a vision, slowly revealed by the dawning light, those soldiers lying on their backs, blood trickling from their mouths; one of the worst atrocities of the war for the beardless Italian soldier called up in the Autumn of 1917. And what of the song of the Fascist squads that ended with a promise of "bombs, bombs / and the dagger's caress". And the multiple stabbing of Matteotti.

"The dagger's caress": how can you accept, help, applaud a faction that promises such things to those who reject it?

FIVE

One might also formulate a "detective-story" hypothesis, which on the one hand aggravated the notion of premeditation, on the other gave the benefit of the doubt about the wickedness of the defendant, which seemed so profound, stubborn and unfathomable. It went like this: that his use of the dagger was prompted not by wickedness, but by a wish to experience the pleasure of killing close to, in a sort of deadly intimacy. Having "envisaged" three killings, at different places and times, he may have reckoned that shooting, at the first or second, might have attracted attention that would prevent him from completing the slaughter "envisaged". He could have used the pistol for the third, but, granted that he had also "envisaged" the place where he would commit suicide, then he needed a little time to get there. But the judge had only to glance at this hypothesis for it to evaporate. Perhaps he had thought that nothing remained but suicide, once the slaughter was consummated. But without conviction, as if judging someone else's actions and fate, something quite apart from him, his being, or his being there. For someone else who had done what he had done, the only open door would be suicide, but maybe he saw himself standing over the three bodies as if in one of those foolish photographs of a day's hunting: the slaughter was fulfilled, and in the great hereafter his victims knew the price of opposing him – or at least they had found out at the moment of death. In the dock, between the two carabinieri, he was forever assuming expressions and attitudes that were both swaggering and servile. And these expressions and attitudes moved the judge to seek something in his case akin to what the penal code called "extenuating circumstances of a generic nature". In his swaggering, servile way, the man might be considered the product of an ambience, almost of a whole city, in which servants were allowed a more swaggering style than their masters. "Capital city of Sicily, seat of the King, distinguished by the title of Archbishopric, renowned among all authors, both ancient and modern, for the amenity of its spacious position, the excellence of its citizens ..." And this was the snag, the false note, the *impasse*: the excellence of the citizens. About two thousand noble families, and many of improbable nobility, were concentrated in Sicily in the eighteenth century; and out of 102,106 "souls", if you take away the masters, what souls do you expect the rest to be, if not servants?

In the legal and judicial undergrowth in which everything, in such a city, is indefinably entangled – as a coefficient, pure number, eluding all measure and measurement – the defendant had undeniably wielded a certain power. In those days when accounts and matrimony were both held sacred, his life could not be called irreproachable; and among his peers his temperament was far from gentle. But he had been awarded the cross of *cavaliere della Corona d'Italia*, and he enjoyed the esteem, one might even say familiarity, of magistrates, lawyers and artists. When called to testify in his favour, most of them maintained a cautious approach: they had no complaints, he had always behaved "with deference" towards them. The Mayor of Palermo, however, had more to admit, so he pleaded the burden of his office, or offices, to avoid testifying in court. But the Court issued an order for him to appear: and this was the first sign that they were not going to be impressed by the hierarchy, from the mayor up, or what the Russians apparently call "nomenclatura". So the mayor climbed into the witness-box, swore the oath, and admitted that he addressed the defendant as "my dear fellow", called him "tu", and had insisted on his being included in the roll of honour of NOMI, the National Organisation for the protection of Mothers and Infants: which had a rather macabre ring in the courtroom, considering the defendant had stabbed the mother of his children. And the defendant had been an associate not only of NOMI, at the express demand of the mayor, but also of the Society for the Protection of Animals, of the Italian Red Cross, of the National Artistic Institute of Fashion, of the Fascist Colonial Institute, of the National Tenants' Association, of the "Azzurri di Dalmazia", a National Association of War Volunteers: all this, either to satisfy people, like the mayor, who wanted him on their side; or because he had a mania for joining and holding membership cards. We don't know if he really was an associate of the Sicilian Society for the History of the Fatherland, whose president had nominated him inspector of The Risorgimento Museum: "In view of your evident patriotism, I beg you on behalf of the Board of Directors, to accept the appointment." In short, he had been involved in so many activities; he had had so many friends. And out of the many documents in the investigation, the judge remembered one which stressed his active and ardent pursuit of friendship, presumably not unprofitable, since the real open doors of the city were those which only friendship could open: perhaps it was a report by the carabinieri. The carabinieri! Those ungrammatical reports of theirs, with their shaky spelling and the curiously "posh" courtroom language that seemed to have evolved from memories of Dante or the opera (with words surfacing every now and then from the southern dialects they were trying to disguise and smother): those reports, thought the judge, were the only truths current in Italy. Not all of them and not always, of course: but you could trust almost all of them, almost always. Just to look at the carabinieri gave him a certain childish sense of security. Perhaps it went back to that childhood game in which the world was divided apodictically between cops and robbers, and nobody much wanted to be the robbers. And in the squalid, ill-lit courtroom where everything was so worn and damp that you feared some sort of contagion, and the stale smell made you think of the lives of Inquisition victims that had macerated there, or the macerating and mouldering of documents macerating other human destinies – even in this courtroom the two carabinieri in their grand uniform standing at his shoulders gave him a sense of security and, whenever he glanced round at them, of repose and visual refreshment. Blue, red and silver: vivid colours in this dead and dusty air. And he privately acknowledged a weakness for their grand uniform: again, a childish weakness, but the adult and judge added the bitter rider that it would be difficult – or at least difficult to imagine – for carabinieri in grand uniform to set about torturing their fellow-men.

SIX

From the many friends he had had, from the many relatives he had helped, from the many people who had shown their esteem for him and who, especially of late, had tried to help him hold on to his job, the defendant now listened to cautious testimonies that so distanced him from their lives that they seemed to be making an effort to remember ever having known him. And in this attitude, according to each man's social standing, two sentiments were at play: one was rather ignoble, dictated by the fear of compromising themselves politically; the other an instinctive repugnance and recoil from a man who, in these three murders that had all the appearance of cold premeditation, had proved to be "a beast", as the prosecution lawyers thundered. (*The man-beast of Palermo* would later be the title of Lawyer Filippo Ungaro's protest to the Court of Cassation calling for a review of the verdict.) It hardly needs saying that the first of these two sentiments prompted the people who had something to lose by compromising themselves politically; and the second, almost to the exclusion of the first, those who had little or nothing to lose and simply felt a horror of "the beast".

Although the newspapers gave no information, the time, place and manner of the three killings were known in minute detail, and more besides: things said to be certain which, on the contrary, if not imaginary were at least dubious.

In the murder of the wife, one detail which seemed to the judge dubious and, however he resolved it, extremely disturbing, to the general public had become a terrible certainty: before stabbing her, the defendant had made his wife say her prayers, for a good death, so to speak. But the facts should be reported, briefly at least.

After collecting the dagger from the knife-sharpener, the defendant had hired a car, a Balilla to be precise, and had returned home to tell his wife he was going to Piana degli Albanesi (the Fascists had foolishly changed the name Albanesi to Greci) to collect the children who were staying with relatives. His wife, the defendant maintained, chose to go with him – but according to the Prosecution it was he who invited her to come, which seemed quite probable, if he had already "envisaged" the slaughter and had the dagger with him. During the journey they quarrelled as usual; and since, in his nervous irritation, he had jerked the wheel and bumped a mudguard, they got out of the car, and as his wife went on nagging, the "rash" act occurred. But just as it seemed unlikely that the wife had insisted on accompanying him, so it seemed quite incredible that things had happened as the defendant maintained: the car-owner testified that there was no trace of a bump on the mudguards; and a peasant from Piana had recognised the dead woman as the lady he had seen praying at a roadside shrine. He had been struck by this well-dressed lady on her knees praying while a well-dressed man, a little way off, was strolling about near a car; then, hearing of a body that had been found in that area, he had gone to the police-station at Piana to report what he had seen. The defendant denied it: either because he really had behaved as judge and executioner, pronouncing the death-sentence upon his wife and giving her a chance to put herself right with the hereafter (he was a very devout man; years ago he had had his family dedicated to the Heart of Jesus by a *monsignore*, a sub-cantor at the cathedral); or because he felt that this detail, of a lady kneeling at prayer on a country road, suggested submission on her part rather than a resumption of their quarrel; or because he felt that killing her immediately after seeing her at prayer somehow made his act seem more solemn and barbarous. Or for the last two reasons together. And the judge oscillated between them, desperately wanting to exclude the one the public took to be certain: that he had cruelly communicated the sentence to his wife, cruelly offered her this celestial chance, then cruelly stabbed her.

A striking feature of the second murder was the cold hypocrisy, the lying, the treachery with which poor Speciale, the accountant, had been drawn into the fatal trap. The defendant had called for him at home, with a friendly smile and a credible pretext to go to the office together: and there, face to face, he had stabbed him, then, according to the charge, contrived to lock the office-door from inside and get out by some other door or window (the topographical description in the report was rather confused), thus delaying the discovery of the body long enough for him to strike down Lawyer Bruno, still unaware of what had happened in the office. But in the defendant's mind, as well as a calculated plan, killing Speciale in the office where, he thought, by sly pimping and prodding the man had coaxed Lawyer Bruno to give him the defendant's job, was part of an almost symbolic design, a rite. However, although the offices were deserted at that hour, someone was about: hearing a cry as the man was stabbed to death, he had run up the stairs and bumped into the defendant on his way down; asked what had happened, the latter had answered casually: "A joker", like Hamlet saying as he killed Polonius: "A rat".

The incident had been included in the police report, but it was when he heard it spoken in evidence that this sudden automatic, and in a sense gratuitous, surfacing of Hamlet's riposte seemed to draw the judge almost unconsciously closer to the defendant. The sordid matter of the trial, the brutal and bloody misery of the facts began to lift and take on the guise of tragedy. And why deny it the name of tragedy, if such passions were involved, revealed to the defendant by a ghostly apparition of despair which cried out for vengeance?

Except that the law does not admit such phantoms; it would not even have admitted them in Hamlet's case, if he had found himself on the level of the law, and not above it: which, the judge recalled, was the difference one of his teachers, speaking of Alfieri, had postulated between tragedy and drama: tragedy was what took place in a sphere where law was powerless, drama what was subordinated to the vigour and rigour of the law; not an exhaustive definition, but quite useful academically. The law admits only one phantom, which is madness. Only then does it stand back from the crime, refrain from judgement, leaving it instead to the psychiatrist, and turning the punishment, in theory – for in fact it is quite another matter – into care.

SEVEN

Lawyer Bruno enjoyed considerable authority and prestige in Palermo, as well as being a popular and respected figure. The spectacular pomp of his funeral, to which the coffin of poor Accountant Speciale was admitted, but from which the first victim's was carefully excluded, had been a demonstration of the unanimous affection and grief of the city, and of their unanimous loathing of the author of these atrocities. So when called upon by the Public Prosecutor's office to undertake the official defence of the accused, some lawyers had refused, pleading the ties of friendship and grief that still bound them to the late-lamented Lawyer Bruno. But when the defendant did manage to find a "family lawyer", as they say, why on earth did the latter not make an immediate appeal that the trial should be transferred to an Assize Court away from Palermo, on the grounds of "legittima suspicione" that he would not get a fair hearing at the scene of the crime? And, granted that it was late to plead "legittima suspicione", why on earth did they not call for psychiatric assessment of the defendant at the start of the proceedings? In his submission to the Court of Cassation, Lawyer Ungaro was later to say: "It should be noted that not once in the proceedings did the defence request psychiatric assessment, clearly indicating their conviction that the defendant had throughout retained the ability to understand and to will his actions." A fine argument for the prosecution, but it really does nothing to explain why an appeal so obvious and basic in a trial of this kind, was overlooked or omitted. Whatever judgement a lawyer may nurse in his heart of hearts about the man he has accepted to defend, his duty is precisely to defend him by all the means the law allows.

Considering the defendant felt he had gleaned a fair sprinkling of the law from his time spent in the judicial and notarial mill, the fact that psychiatric assessment was not requested as the hearing went on, more or less convinced the judge it must be the man's own decision. Fierce, twisted and desperate self-love that had gone beyond control. "*Amour propre* lives by all extremes ... it even crosses over to the side of its enemies, enters into their designs, and – in a wonderful way – joins them in hating itself, plots its own destruction, works for its own ruin: in short, is concerned only to exist, and in order to exist, adapts to becoming its own enemy." *In a wonderful way*, says La Rochefoucauld: and taking away from the wonderful its sense of wonder and amazement, the judge gave it the sense of wondering, examining, scrutinizing: which is precisely the role of the psychiatrist. If, then, in his madness, the defendant refused to be relegated to the sphere of madness, the defence could, indeed should, have put forward the request, at the risk of his opposition. But perhaps the defence too had only a common, banal notion of madness: madness without method, without calculation, inconsequential; while there is a sort of madness in which only the first link is faulty, and all the rest is methodical, calculated and consequential, and the first is usually the link of self-love in relation to an enemy.

"One must also bear in mind", thought the judge, "that whether it was refused by the defendant or neglected by the defence, the very fact of applying for psychiatric assessment at this stage, even if the Court accepted it, would provoke a storm of derision in the prosecution ranks and in public opinion, which might prejudice the result ... But the fact remains that this man lacks the two elements that should have been the mainstay of the defence: 'legittima suspicione', that defence lawyers often prefer to call 'an atmosphere of raging passion', and psychiatric assessment." And so, thinking over the technicalities of the trial, and linking certain moments in it with things he had read, or thought about things he had read, the little judge drew imperceptibly closer to the defendant, to his fierce, twisted humanity, to his madness; in short, as was his duty, seeing him with painful clarity.

One thing that troubled him somewhat was the part played in all this by his own aversion to Fascism (even if he refused to consider himself an anti-Fascist, merely opposing to Fascism his personal dignity in thought and action). He could not fail to recognise that if, instead of Lawyer Bruno, one of the three victims had been a cousin of the defendant (they had always hated each other), or just any other clerk in the office, the trial would have proceeded aseptically in a more or less routine way, though still involving for him, of course, the problem of not leading to the death penalty. But Lawyer Bruno belonged to a corporation, and was its chief representative in the provinces: the corporation must inevitably rise up with all its might and means to bring down the maximum penalty upon the guilty person, Fascism or no Fascism. Any corporation will react with exasperation against any threat to its security, even in the sphere of opinion; just imagine the reaction to a criminal attack against a corporation, like lawyers (or judges), whose natural habitat is law. So the corporate closing of ranks against the defendant was perfectly natural and spontaneous, and would have occurred even in a free system. But in fact, it was a Fascist idea, at the core of Fascist thinking, that the death penalty was, so to speak, an innate part of its existence, its security and its defence, suspended over any possible opposition and ready, before or beyond judgement, to fall upon anyone who offended the party in any way. Thus, after about forty years, the death penalty had been reintroduced in Italy, in defence of the Fascist state, and had been imposed upon those intending, simply intending, an attempt upon the life of Mussolini. Then it had been extended to the most serious non-political crimes, but the political stamp remained so that the solemn funeral ordained by the Fascist organisations, and by the party itself, then the appoint-

ment as Counsel for the Prosecution of the honourable
Doctor Alessandro Pavolini, in the name and interests of the
Fascist Confederation of Professionals and Artists, these were
already a death sentence for the defendant, the Assize Court
being summoned only as a matter of form and ceremony.
And in all this the judge recognised that his aversion to Fascism played a part, and rightly so; but he tried to contain it,
telling himself it was not altogether true, if, as judge in this
trial, he was consulting only his own conscience and his own
"dignity". But each day increased a sense, like an indefinable
(all too clearly definable) threat, of isolation and growing
solitude. A question from his wife had made it painful to the
point of obsession. They had never discussed his work, that
weight of papers and scruples he carried with him even at
home, in the hours he spent shut away in his study among his
books. So he was startled by the sudden question, one day at
table: "Will he be condemned?" She certainly meant would he
be condemned to death: fearing he would, he chose to think.
But the suspicion that she, like all the rest, felt it was right
that he should die and that any other verdict would be an
absolution, gnawed at him insidiously, especially as she
looked reassured and appeased when he replied: "Of course,
he will."

EIGHT

There was, however, in the jury drawn for this trial, in a few of the jurors (the law at that time required that they should be called assessors), some scarcely perceptible sign of human tenderness. Not towards the defendant – none could rise to that – but towards life, the things of life, its order and disorder. As with the homosexuals in a famous page of Proust – though here it had nothing to do with homosexuality – it is given to some happy or unhappy men, in sensitivity, intelligence, and in their thoughts, to meet, recognise and choose each other.

Five selected jurors, one substitute. Three were tradesmen, and betrayed their anxiety for the business they had left with others for the sake of the trial; occasionally they lamented the fact. Of the others, one was a municipal clerk, one a teacher of Latin and Greek in a grammar-school, one a farmer. These three were selected members, as were two of the tradesmen, one of whom, despite an absent look apparently intent upon following from afar what was going on in the "colonial grocer's", as they were then called, which his wife and son were running in his absence, also had a sharp ear and quick understanding for what was going on in the court. But the other four were attentive too, quietly attentive, and shrewd. The substitute, on the other hand, showed a certain inattention and impatience, an occasional spasm of boredom; he felt useless and as if trapped there by a whim of the presiding judge.

With three of them – the "colonial" grocer, the farmer and the teacher – the judge had established a rapport, an afflatus, an understanding: over and above the few words they exchanged every day and one might even say through the silences their eyes exchanged every now and then, during the hearings and in the meetings in the council chamber. Especially with the farmer. He had the tanned face of a peasant, large peasant hands, a peasant's proverbs and metaphors: but one day the judge heard him talking to the teacher about the codex of *Daphnis and Chloe* at the Laurenziana, and the blot of ink Courier had left on it.* Sometimes, for some people, the name of a writer, the title of a book, can ring out like the name of one's homeland: this was the effect on the judge of the name of Courier, in whose *Complete Works*, found in the lumber-room of a relative who did not know what to do with them, he had begun to spell out French and logic, French and law.

One day towards the end of the trial, when he got home, the door-porter gave him an envelope that seemed to contain a card: a large sealed envelope, with neither his name nor that of the bearer or sender on it. "He told me it was for you, but he wouldn't say from whom ... I insisted, but he said you knew." And as if by way of apology: "He looked a decent Christian fellow ... Tall, face like a peasant; dresses like a farmer in his Sunday best." Like all those born in a back alley in Palermo, the porter felt a certain scorn for country people, even if he considered them, more for the simplicity of their minds than for the piety of their lives, decent Christians. The judge knew who it was. And when he opened the envelope and looked inside, good Christian seemed a fair definition of the bearer: between two pieces of card was an old popular woodcut. Nothing else: not a note, not a word. It was a picture of a Madonna, crowned by two angels, between two saints, one of whom was clearly Saint John. The group was ethereal, radiating shafts of light, held up by clouds that, to tell the truth, looked like shapeless lumps of stone. Below were a little church, a bridge with two small trees, four figures praying in the flames of purgatory, a guillotine, a gallows with a man dangling from it, and the words: *The Society of the Souls of the Beheaded*. The judge remembered: the image referred to one of the most obscure and spontaneous cults that had grown up in the Catholic Church in Sicily at a certain moment: never officially encouraged, perhaps, but certainly widely tolerated. Tolerance for the souls of the beheaded had reached the point that the word "holy" had slipped in, and the cult of the souls in purgatory had merged with that of the souls of the beheaded: "the holy souls of the beheaded", an expression not admitted and not seen in writing, but predominant in common speech and common worship. Indeed, in the village where he was born, and to which he returned every holiday, the judge remembered the little Church of the Holy Souls, very much like the one in the woodcut. It must have been built for the holy souls in purgatory – all the inhabitants of the village through the centuries, since nobody would admit that even the most distant of his forbears could be anywhere in the hereafter but in purgatory; but at some point the souls of the beheaded had begun to take possession, so that the little church, at the end of the inhabited world, inspired those who approached it after dark with terrifying visions of beheaded (head in hand) and hanged men, and the fact that these spectres were guardian spirits, preserving passers-by to whom they appeared from all violence, did not stop them causing such terror as to make the hair stand on end, or even turn white.

The movement towards such a cult must have started in the second half of the sixteenth century, when the Compagnia dei Bianchi was formed to comfort the condemned, praying with them to the last, then continuing to intercede for their souls with prayers and masses. Considering that the condemned were at first denied any religious consolation, the history of religion had taken a step forward. As had the history of Reason, since one Palermo writer, like Guicciardini leaving "memoirs" to his children, particularly recommended a son who was entering upon a legal career not to prescribe torture or flogging, and never to condemn to death "for anything whatsoever".

And now the judge had gone searching in the disorder of his many books for the little volume of *Christian Admonitions* by Argisto Giuffredi, written five or six years before his tragic death in 1591.* He found the passage at once, as he had folded down the corner of the page about ten years before. "I know full well", said Giuffredi, "that this will seem to you an extravagant opinion"; and it certainly must have seemed so, two centuries before Beccaria.* How had Giuffredi arrived at that "extravagant" idea? Speaking of the most common torture of the time, the rope, he states his reason quite clearly: "for that, apart from the danger a man is put in, by confessing, of dying, he is also put in danger of breaking his neck, by, as I have sometimes seen, the breaking of the rope or the beam to which it is attached: and be advised that today this use of the rope has come to such a pass that, where formerly it was not applied unless with those evidences or testimonies which today, as if certain proofs, incur the ultimate penalty: the rope is now ordered for such shallow evidences that it is a disgrace ..." Giuffredi evidently feared the effects of torture on the innocent: perhaps because he too had been an innocent victim of torture, we do not know on what accusation, and had been on the point of confessing guilt ; and as for the disgrace of resorting to it too freely, the judge thought: "just like today, in the squads of the *polizia giudiziaria*: and it is a disgrace, for us judges." And Giuffredi's radical aversion to capital punishment followed naturally upon his aversion to torture and flogging, but perhaps there was another reason, private and more anguished: the condemning to death, perhaps innocently, of a beautiful lady who held a sort of literary salon in the town, and with whom Giuffredi, as a young man, may have been in love. (If not, why had the other Palermo poets dedicated to him the verses they wrote upon the death of the beautiful lady?)

He left his reading of Giuffredi to look for another book he had suddenly remembered: by Pitrè, on the cult of the souls of the beheaded.* He had always loved to unravel a thread of spontaneous curiosity through his books and in his thoughts, ever since he had had dealings with books: which was why his brothers, whose relations with books required will-power and effort, thought him a time-waster. But he knew how much he had gained from those wasted hours and days; and anyway, he had always taken pleasure in it.

Here was the Pitrè: twenty pages, all about that cult. But he gave no answer to the questions why. Why in Sicily, why in that century, why the contradiction of flocking to the so-called judgements as if to festivals, then conferring sanctity on the condemned? He began to answer his own questions: but we leave it to each reader to seek his own answers.

NINE

A few years before, a grand celebration in honour of great Sicilians had been ordained by the regime: one of those contradictions forced upon Fascism by its need in some respect to come to terms with the reality, the history and the habits of the Italians. They were opposed to regionalism, but so that certain regions should not feel forgotten – as indeed they were – they set about exalting the men who were born there and who in spite of being born there, greater and lesser alike, had been blissfully indifferent to the birthplace, or had held a distinctly low opinion of it. Sicily had not realised she had so many great sons: visiting academics from mainland Italy came to remind her. But she continued in ignorance of Argisto Giuffredi, whose greatness consisted chiefly in a private "memoir" against torture, public corporal punishment and the death penalty: a "memoir" which had emerged in 1896 from an archive manuscript, but which must certainly not be remembered at a time when Italy was full of such pernicious nonsense as this by an idealist philosopher: "even death may be considered not in vain, if it has given or restored to the guilty man one hour, one moment of that contact with the infinite that he had lost." A stupendous notion, that might perhaps have suggested to a tyrant like Phalaris (see Diodorus Siculus)★ the murderous whim of putting that philosopher in contact with infinity right away; but Mussolini's tyranny consisted of less murderous, quite modest caprices. It is worth remembering the pun on Plato and platoon by the sculptor and wit Marino Mazzacurati, when he dubbed an idealist philosopher who later went over to Marxism (without ever, I suspect, losing sight of his contact with the infinite): "Il Platone d'esecuzione". And he, alas, was not the only Plato turned executioner, nor could one say that the line of such philosophers has ended.

But to return to the judge: the day after the anonymous gift of the woodcut, as he was donning his robe and the jurors their tricolour sashes, he asked the farmer in an absent-minded way: "Do you know Giuffredi's *Christian Admonitions?*" Looking slightly embarrassed and confused, the juror said he did. And to make the signal more explicit, the judge added: "I re-read some passages yesterday, and then a chapter of Pitrè's *Customs and Usages.*" The juror nodded, as if approving his reading–matter.

That morning there was to be some excitement in the courtroom. As we have seen, the Public Prosecutor's Office had insisted that the police produce the picture of Matteotti found in the defendant's house. But now they had got it, the very fact of their insistence upon having it put them in the thorny position of having to confront the defendant with it. And he was perhaps more frightened of this than of the impending penalty for three murders confessed in all their "envisaging": clearly, and with the most damning effect, he could think of nothing better than lying.

The minutes on the interrogation had already been closed, but the Prosecutor, who had havered about it, obviously decided at the last minute to go ahead, which meant that the clerk, after writing "read, confirmed and signed", had added: "and before the signing, the defendant stated in answer to a question: 'It is true there may have been a photograph of Giacomo Matteotti in my house. It was passed on to me by Bruno long after the Matteotti episode was closed. In fact, this is how it came into my hands: from time to time he used to give me all the magazines and papers he no longer needed, which might include anything sent to his office: advertisements for hotels, invitations to conferences, etc. One day this photo of Matteotti was in the bundle. I took them home, and forgot all about it.'" The Prosecutor did not pursue the matter; he had achieved his object: that the politicians should not say he had failed to understand the gravity of keeping a picture of Matteotti in the house, and those still attached to legality should not say he had failed to understand the law. As if to say: I have taken note of the matter, but cannot turn it into a charge; the Assize Court judges can deal with it as they choose, or as best they can. Just two links in the chain of transferring and off-loading responsibility, which, for people whose lives are entangled in the Italian judicial system, tends to be an endless one, coming to resemble in some cases the idealist philosopher's contact with infinity.

The Assize Court dealt with it according to the law; the picture of Matteotti could not be considered criminal evidence; moreover, the fact that the defendant kept it at home had not even been mentioned as a crime in the case for the prosecution. It was as if the Prosecutor had asked for it out of some personal, private curiosity. That it added a further count of grave and offensive amorality against the defendant was an opportunity the prosecution did not let slip. But judges, lawyers on both sides and spectators at the trial alike had no doubt about the truth of the matter: in his mania for joining, belonging, siding with anything that was, or might shortly become, powerful, the defendant, like the keen lotto player he was, had played the number of Fascism on the wane and Socialism on the rebound; and in his mania for hoarding, had kept the picture of Matteotti when it had become not only a losing card, but dangerous enough to ruin a man and cost him his freedom and his job. Political exile; instant dismissal by the state authorities, without gratuity or pension. The judge remembered a case very close to him: a distant relative who had lost his job as an elementary school-master, and had been unable to get another because he gave a lira towards the Matteotti monument in the summer of 1924, and had been given that photo as a sort of receipt. A man of fifty, he would drift silently round the house, and only the name of Mussolini would provoke, as a conditioned reflex, the exclamation: "That murderer has ruined me."

TEN

All the jurors wore the Fascist badge in their buttonholes, but if you had asked any one of them in confidence if he felt he was a Fascist, he would have answered with a hesitant yes; and if you had asked again even more confidentially, among friends, and adding "really", it is likely that one of them would have given an outright no, while the others would have avoided a yes: not out of caution, but in all sincerity. They had never faced up to the problem of judging Fascism as a whole, just as they had never judged Catholicism. They had been baptised and confirmed, had arranged baptisms and confirmations, had got married in Church (those that were married), and had sent for the priest for dying relatives. And they carried a Fascist card and wore a Fascist badge. But there were plenty of things they disapproved of in the Catholic Church. And plenty in Fascism. Catholics, Fascists. But while the Catholic Church stood there, massive and firm as a rock, so that they could always call themselves Catholics in the same way, Fascism did not: it was always in a state of flux, changing, and changing their – ever decreasing – sense of being Fascists. It was happening all over Italy for most Italians. Acceptance of the Fascist regime, which had been solid for at least ten years, was beginning to crack and weaken. The conquest of Ethiopia was all very well: though they couldn't understand how on earth a conquered empire meant, for the conquerors, a growing shortage of things that had been plentiful, at least for those who could afford them. And then, why on earth had Mussolini got involved in the Spanish war and in an ever-closer friendship with Hitler? Although they went on repeating, more and more wearily, the hyperbole about sleeping with open doors, it was the open door of the Brenner Pass that was beginning to worry them: even if armies were not about to pour through it, looting and laying waste, it seemed as if veritable flocks of ill-omen were already sweeping through. The fact was, things were going from bad to worse. And the "quiet life" to which people had anxiously aspired for centuries, was beginning to appear ever more remote and unattainable. The Fascist party was becoming more and more obliging to its insiders, and harsher to outsiders. And this impatience, widespread throughout Italy at different levels of awareness, was active at different levels in the six jurors too, although it had little to do with the trial, except, somewhat tenuously, for the fact that the death penalty had always been considered Fascist, and, more tenaciously, for the fact that it was required in this case, for this man, not only because his crimes were punishable by death, but also because one of the victims had represented municipal Fascism and an important section of the Fascist corporations – the most important in Palermo for prestige, if not in number. The corporation, and Fascism, were summed up in one name: Alessandro Pavolini, who had accepted the role of plaintiff for the corporation in this trial, and was one of the best known figures in Fascism, after commanding an air squadron called "the dare-devils" in the Ethiopian war.* We cannot know if Pavolini felt a shiver of presentiment, as he followed the Palermo trial from home – as it seems he did – then in the Court of Cassation, and then in the Appeal Court: a presentiment that he too would find himself standing, as he wished the defendant to do, before a firing-squad.

But, with one quite certain exception, at the beginning of the trial all the jurors were in favour of capital punishment in the abstract: for reasons, as the Prosecutor had seen so clearly, of open doors. But in each man this abstract consensus underwent modifications and moderations in the course of argument which, if they did not end up in a denial, came quite close to it. Common to all was the affirmation that some people, for certain crimes of peculiar savagery or for despicable motives, *deserved it*. But between the consideration that they deserved it and the necessity of carrying it out, began the divergence of opinions, particularly in relation to judicial error. Those who remained in favour, either considering error to be unlikely, seeing how such trials were bound to get at the truth, or accepting the risk fairly cynically, nevertheless stopped in perplexity at that sort of borderline where the problem ceased to be abstract and general, and became quite concretely particular and personal. The death penalty is law, there are criminals who deserve it: "but is it really my business to decide whether they deserve it and then to impose it?" To those who experienced it, this perplexity seemed to imply they were only one step away from questioning the very existence of lay juries: but only where the death sentence was concerned; and an assurance by the professional judges, in their robes, that the penalty was necessary and inevitable, would have sufficed to appease it. And it should be said at this point that for southerners, of any southern clime, a judge, a man who chooses the job of judging his fellow-men, is a comprehensible figure if he is corrupt, but a man of unfathomable sentiments and intentions, as if detached from common human feeling, in short incomprehensible, if he does not allow himself to be corrupted by material things or by friendship or by compassion. As Don Quixote said as he freed the galley-slaves: let everyone answer for his sins in the other world (up or down), but it is not right that down (or up) here men of honour should appoint themselves judges of others who have done them no harm; but we may add, setting aside Don Quixote, if there are men who beyond or above the matter of honour, have chosen to judge other men, let them answer for their sins or merits in the other world (up or down): but a man who did not choose to judge and who, all unprepared, relies upon their knowledge and expertise, has nothing to answer for in the hereafter, up or down. A state of mind that may apply, from a minimum to a maximum according – Savinio would say – to the thickness of their overcoats, to all juries: but certainly to most of the jurors in the trial we are talking about. Not that such a state of mind made them inattentive to the proceedings; indeed, in their preoccupation with the responsibility they would ultimately have to assume, they would have been more inattentive, if they had felt themselves to be judges, as in fact they were, on a par with the ones in robes.

They had reacted indignantly to the defendant's lie about the picture of Matteotti: as a prosecuting lawyer put it, it was a second stab in the heart of poor Lawyer Bruno: in the heart of his sure and limpid Fascist faith; but the opinion of the judges in their robes that the detail of the picture was irrelevant to the trial calmed the fears of some that outside the courtroom, in the eyes of the party they belonged to, it might appear extremely grave, and that their dismissal of the fact that the defendant, in hatred of Fascism, had kept this portrait for more than ten years might have serious consequences for them.

ELEVEN

The jurors who had wives were questioned about the trial every day by their wives, and their evasive answers, broken phrases and incomprehensible mutterings led to resentment and reproofs. The jurors kept the secret they had sworn: it cost them to remain silent with friends, but in their heart of hearts they approved the law which bound them to silence with their wives. The two be-robed judges and the Public Prosecutor also had to adopt a shield of silence, or resort to vague replies. And all the ladies' questions, insinuated or direct, could be summed up in the one asked by our judge's wife: "Will he be condemned?"; that is, to death, since any other sentence seemed to them inadequate for a man who had so cruelly killed his wife. The other two crimes were terrible, it's true: but murdering his wife ... Housewives at that time, who really stayed at home, bound by rules and habits that a girl of twenty today could not possibly imagine applying to her and to her life, felt in a vague sort of way that everything outside the home was Fascism, that spies and informers were lying in wait on all sides, starting from the door-porter's lodge in the block of flats, to catch the lukewarm, the grumblers and, a category particularly hated by the regime, the indifferent. And since almost all Italians, and therefore their husbands, belonged to one of those three categories, or to all three according to the mood and the moment, they feared this trial was a sort of acid test to find them more or less lacking in zeal: and then inscrutable sanctions would descend upon them, ruining the whole family. So frustrated curiosity mixed with apprehenson prevailed in the minds of the jurors' wives, equal curiosity but greater apprehension in the judges' wives: but the wife of the Public Prosecutor settled for curiosity, certain as she was that her husband would call for the death penalty. For her, therefore, no anxiety that this trial would put an end to her husband's career and bring him into such disfavour with the whole party hierarchy as to disrupt his work, his social life, and the fairly serene course of his family life; which is what the two judges' wives more specifically feared. But it is only fair to say that the ladies, who were then kept out of so many things (above, below), saw the death penalty in images, words and music that had more to do with the rare treat of going to the theatre or the cinema than with reality and conscience: André Chénier, Mario Cavaradossi,★ Maximilian of Austria in an American film, and so on from guillotine to firing squad, from innocent condemned aristocrats to some convict on whom repentance and resignation conferred the nobility that the idealist philosopher called "contact with the infinite".

"Don't talk of rope in a hanged man's house, or even in the house of the hangman", a Polish writer would say about ten years later; and it could be said that talking about this case, for those who were close to it or felt close to it, was rather like being in the house of the hanged man and the hangman at one and the same time: whatever the intensity or awareness of such feelings, the direct or inverse ratio of the two terms. It was for this reason too, above all others, that those standing close to the abyss shrank from discussing it, however vaguely, with anyone who could not see what an abyss it was – for their conscience and for their life. It was not only a problem of justice – administering it according to the law, or affirming it against the law; it was also a problem of inner freedom, which is the prerogative of anyone called upon to judge.

Outside the hearings, therefore, they tried, not only not to talk about it, which was easy, but not to think about it, which was extremely difficult. And the fact that the jurors tried to meet up, as if casually or upon pretexts connected with their regular activities, was the reverse side of the same coin. Of the two judges, ours also felt the need, one Sunday, to meet the juror whose occupation was farming, and accept his invitation to spend a few hours in the country. "Without a thought in the world": which was impossible, since even letting your eye travel over the countryside, picking out a tree or a stone, is already a thought. Even if it is not *that* thought.

It was a mild, opulent, golden November, as always in Palermo. Although the Feast of the Faithful Departed was over, the pastryshop windows were bright with gingerbread men and marzipan fruits, just as Indian figs, sorb-apples in wadding, date-plums and oranges brightened the fruit-stalls. "Presents from the dead", gingerbread men and marzipan fruits, that children seek and find in some corner of the house on the 2nd of November: and in bed the night before they had stayed awake just a few minutes longer than usual, feigning sleep, in the hope of seeing the dead arrive with the gifts and hide them; not a bit afraid, for these were family dead, some of whom even the children had known quite recently. The dead bringing gifts; mass-produced killing among the living; those stalls offering bread and cheese as well as fruit on a Sunday, when selling was forbidden; the price-tickets on the goods that you thought meant kilos, but when you got closer, putting on your glasses if necessary, you discovered meant half-kilos; the police with a carton of fruit in their hands instead of a note-book for fines: all things that combined to give the judge the sense of a city beyond redemption.

The tram had reached the outskirts of the town. At the stop where the country began, open and green with orange-groves, the judge got off. He had suddenly decided not to go to the juror's villa. There was no rule, written or customary, that disallowed personal contact or an exchange of visits between judge and juror; but he had suddenly made one for himself. "When the trial is over," he thought, for he was curious about this country-house, the library the juror had spoken of, his way of life. He walked home, in a city in its Sunday best, with bright dresses that were beginning daringly to reveal the flesh and outline the forms of the ladies walking arm-in-arm with their soberly dressed husbands and fiancés, and where cabs blossomed with ladies' cloche hats. "Daydreaming my dry-as-dust thoughts", he mused about himself, and about his thinking, on the contrary, the most fluid of thoughts. Dreaming, too, about this line of poetry, and failing to recall who wrote it.

TWELVE

The trial went its predictable way, except for the defendant's adding to it an element seriously damaging to himself. Obvious lies; expressions that slipped out, in references to his three victims, betraying in- extinguishable hatred. Not a shade of repentance or remorse: he just went on calling his murderous acts "rash".

He had tried to cast on Bruno the suspicion that he had dismissed him, not for petty thefts, which were the result of book-keeping audits and which he himself had admitted as quite pardonable trivia, but in competition for the favours an office-typist had granted him and denied to Bruno: something he had once boasted of, but which he now declared was a false impression on Bruno's part, swearing that the behaviour of the typist in question was beyond reproach. He probably saw this as the conduct of a man of honour and a gentleman: but it did not stop the poor lady, now living her life in a small town far away, from being called to testify, resulting in such damage as the news, even if unreported by the papers in their general silence about the whole trial, must inevitably cause as it passed from mouth to mouth throughout the length of Italy from Palermo to the small town she was living in.

Then he tried to cast another suspicion on Bruno: that he had attempted to seduce his wife, having gone to his house at least twice in his absence. And when asked if he had also suspected his wife of responding to Bruno's somewhat sporadic attentions, he had replied that he did not think so: but in the same style and tone of voice as when he denied the relations he had boasted with the typist. Like a gentleman who replied with a no which should be interpreted as a yes, out of sheer generosity. Which aroused such indignation that the President repeated, *sotto voce*, what the prosecution had said of the Matteotti portrait he claimed to have had from Bruno: that he was stabbing his wife all over again. And I've just noticed that I have spoken for the first time of the President of the Court: this was not the one I sometimes call the little judge, or our judge. The judge we have been talking about from the first was what is usually called – perhaps inaccurately as regards its meaning in the courts – the *giudice a latere* or associate-judge: but more formidable than the President (or less, for everything is relative) in his expertise, as a man of letters (which counted at that time in any profession), and for his acute and unfettered judgement. The President was a solemn, silent man, rigorous in his conduct of a trial and of this particular trial, impenetrable in his thoughts and feelings even about those closest to him; perhaps the impenetrability was his answer to a certain awe he felt for his *a latere*, to whom he was shrewdly giving plenty of room.

But even if, as he (you might well say, rashly) hoped, the defendant had succeeded in persuading people that Lawyer Bruno had given him the Matteotti picture in a bundle of papers, that he was jealous because the typist resisted his advances, or that he had attempted to dishonour him as head of a family, these were not the sort of things to impeach the memory of the late-lamented Lawyer Bruno. He might rather be blamed for his prolonged indulgence about the cash-leaks, his long-standing tolerance of the petty but continual embezzling: indeed, if he were alive the law would have gone beyond blaming him, but now that he was dead, at the hand of the man who had long profited by his indulgence, there had been a sort of tacit agreement to emphasise his kindness and generosity as opposed to the monstrous and brutal ingratitude of his murderer. But it was precisely his kindness and indulgence – thought the judge – that had been his undoing, unleashing the fury of the defendant when they came to an end, as end they must: he had been tolerated so long, he could not see why this tolerance should fail him at that particular moment. And Bruno had been warned of his underling's viewpoint, and of his threats, by colleagues who apparently tried to persuade him to go on ignoring and forgiving. But Bruno had answered the more explicit threats reported by one man with a careless: "What will he do then – kill me?" either because he was resolved to do his duty, or because he thought the man too meek ever to do what, in fact, he promptly did. Or for both reasons: and the defence quibbled in vain about the second, for the man's meekness, admitting he had been meek in the past, became quite incredible in view of his determination, his weapon, and the way the three crimes were committed; not to mention his conduct in the courtroom, always an important factor in criminal trials, which could not be said to arouse the remotest desire to understand or pity him.

And this is the reason – the judge's thoughts went on – why things will always go to the bad in this world: personal relations, friendly interventions and recommendations, compassion for the innocent who might suffer in the punishment of the guilty, settling for the lesser evil in view of the greater that might result from revealing it; in short, (like Manzoni's count-uncle and the country priest in league with him), blocking and smoothing over anything that might involve the law, for fear of consequences that might prove of vast and serious import, but not so vast and serious in the long run as letting things be, tolerating, paying to friendship a tribute of silences and omissions. It all comes to this. Or almost all.

THIRTEEN

Only at the final stages, in the flood of "concluding state-ments", did the counsel for the defence launch his appeal for an assessment of the defendant's capacity to comprehend and to will his acts: and they were not arguing insanity but partial insanity: a man divided between sense and madness, with sense prevailing over madness at times or – and certainly at the moment of the crime – madness over sanity. "The man who commits a crime in a state of total insanity is not punish-able ... The man who commits a crime in a state of partial insanity must answer for the crime, but the penalty is dimi-nished." But in the case in question it would have been easier to plead total than partial insanity: as in any criminal trial in our opinion. For in every human being partial insanity, or something technically indefinable of that kind (admitting that partial insanity itself is a valid technical term) is sleeping or lying in wait, and therefore liable to start awake or to explode at the right moment (that is, at the wrong, most ill-fated moment); so to refer to it and recognise it in certain crimes of passion, and not in all, is ultimately to proclaim that inequa-lity of the law that popular opinion considers intrinsic to its functioning, as opposed to the principle declaring it to be equal for all.

Anyway, it was too late. One might well ask if the defence lawyer should not have tried to persuade the defendant to agree to the request, entrenched as he seemed, and in his folly really was, in the belief that he had only taken his revenge for wrongs suffered a little too far. They were in the council chamber now, which as regards décor was no less disagreeable, in the visual and olfactory sense, than the audience chamber. On walls that had been whitewashed before the law courts were established there, drawings and writings left by two centuries of victims of the Inquisition could be seen through the coat of lime, or were revealed where it had flaked away. They were partly covered by wooden shelves with their serried ranks of pamphlets, but some writings and drawings could be seen in full. By now the judges knew them very well, some to the point of obsession; but the jurors looked at them curiously. And some felt a sense of dismay to find themselves administering secular law, albeit weighed down with ancient curbs and patched up with modern mysticism, in the very rooms in which it had been tenaciously and fanatically denied.

The council chamber. And as the judges donned and doffed their robes there, and the jurors their tricolour sashes, with the portraits on the walls and the mouldy smell of old papers, it made one think of a sacristy. In a more fundamental sense, too, by virtue of the ritual they had come forth to celebrate each morning, and of the final ritual they were preparing, which would sum up all that so many sessions had revealed about the defendant's life and actions. He had, as it were, been stripped bare. His cult of the family, which he displayed above all by insisting, against his wife's wishes, on bringing two unmarried sisters to live with them, was non-existent. As a married man he had seduced a thirteen-year-old girl, and set her up in a house in Palermo, where he kept her and had children by her. It was also charged to his account that, as a young boy, he had run away with the girl he had then married – the classic "flit" of poor youngsters – surrendering to marriage after being denounced by her father for abduction of a minor and unlawful sexual intercouse. As for his patriotism, he had kept out of the front line in the 1915 war, possibly by means of a self-inflicted wound. His meekness: he had been involved in violent quarrels, always carried a gun, and taught his sons that a pistol was more important than bread. His devotion to work: he stole from the petty-cash and held back the subscriptions the lawyers paid to be included in the album of honour. And then there were the crimes of that "grim" day. The murder of his wife was totally premeditated, for in a testament-letter to his sons, written at least a year before and found among his papers, he said he wanted to "put her down": a veterinary expression intended to refer to his wife's animality, but which rebounded to suggest a bestiality of his own. And he had been able to carry out the three murders because the victims and the people around them had trusted him. He had invited his wife to go for a drive to pick up their children. He had called to ask Speciale, the accountant, to accompany him to the Palace of Justice to look for a file he needed urgently. He had been shown into Lawyer Bruno's house by the maid, as a friend. Three times in a matter of hours he had taken the dagger, well sharpened for the purpose, from its case: and with a steady hand, presumably looking them in the eye, perhaps enjoying the moment of final torture he was inflicting on them, he had plunged it into the bodies of his victims. Twice, which seemed to the judges and jurors the most atrocious detail, he had put the bloody dagger back in its case, and the last time thrown it at Lawyer Bruno's niece who was following him downstairs. That was the moment when he could have used the pistol in his pocket against himself, as he said he had planned: not only did he not do so, but meeting his wife's brother at the police station, where he was immediately taken, he warned the police to see if he was armed, fearing that he might succumb to the urge to avenge his sister. Another detail that made a deep impression on the judges and jurors, and seemed to sum up his character.

But after quite a short discussion, the Court emerged from the Council Chamber with a verdict which was not the death sentence.

FOURTEEN

About ten days later, while most people were still in a state of shock and resentment about this verdict, and a few – colleagues, lawyers and party leaders – raised a bitter, accusatory "I told you so" against the associate judge, meaning that he was not a Fascist and that he had shown contempt for the regime; about ten days later, then, the little judge decided he would go and call on the juror, who had an old villa at the gates of the town. I see I have called him the little judge again, not because he was particularly small in stature, but because of the impression I retained of him from the first time I saw him. He was in a group of men and, pointing him out as the shortest among them, someone said to me: "He had a brilliant career ahead of him, but he ruined it by refusing to condemn a man to death"; and he gave me a rather sketchy account of the trial. From then on, every time I saw him, and on the few occasions I spoke to him, it seemed a measure of his greatness to call him small: because of the things so much more powerful than himself that he had confronted with serenity.

So he went to the villa, one December day shortly before Christmas: a day as warm as September. Even in the suburbs the city already had a festive air, but of a Christmas still unaware of the northern fir-tree and presents, content with the crib, the capon, dried figs and roasted almonds.

He found the house easily enough: it stood as if within the walls of a little fort, and you could see the apex of its neo-classical pediment from a distance. But the building was not entirely neo-classical, for there had been alterations, additions and more additions; there was even a stupendous Chiaramonti two-light window, like the ones in The Steri in which justice was celebrated.

The owner of the house greeted him like an old friend he had not seen for some time; and that is how the judge felt: that they had not seen each other for a long time. The days that had passed since the verdict, with all that had been said and all that they had thought, seemed to have expanded. And now they met again like people who had once lived through a dramatic experience together, and escaped a danger; and they almost felt a sense of mutual gratitude for the help they had given each other in the escape. They had both been in the war, at the same age and almost the same places, perhaps they had met, even spoken to each other, so they felt as if they were coming out of it now as companions and friends, while the air still throbbed with resentful threatening comments about the verdict. But they both tried not to mention the trial. In fact they talked about the war, and their memories. And then about books, sitting in the fine library: a spacious, harmonious room, warm with the colours of the shelves, and with a real grace in the decorations and the carvings that touched upon the rococo and anticipated Art Nouveau.

The judge was fascinated by this man with the antique peasant face, and great peasant hands opening books and leafing through them with impressive delicacy, dressed in corduroy velvet which was the peasants' Sunday best at the time (but on a closer look proved to be of a different quality and cut).

While he was showing the judge one of the books lying on the table, the Bodoni from the Camera della Badessa that had arrived that morning, he said: "Perhaps you imagine this house has come down to me through a long family line, but the fact is I don't even know what my great-grandfather did, but he certainly lived in such miserly poverty that his son, my grandfather, thought of nothing but building up miserly wealth. All this comes from him, from my grandfather: he got it from some member of a great family who was deeply in debt to him. With the library as it stands, or almost; I've added maybe a sixth of the books that you see. Mostly nineteenth and twentieth century French, many of them in the fine editions the French are so clever at, and that we are just making timid attempts at producing. Illustrated books, a weakness of mine: to make up for a childhood in which I longed for an illustrated *Pinocchio* or an illustrated *Cuore*★ with a passion equal to the obstinacy of my grandfather's refusal to buy me them. He was illiterate, he hated books: fortunately he died before he could carry out his plan of getting rid of all these. Don't think I'm a cynic to say fortunately: I don't remember my father, and, all things considered, I can say I was quite fond of my grandfather, in spite of the fear of him that I got from my mother. A rough diamond. As for the debts paid for with this house, the canon who was his father-confessor assured me there was no usury involved; but I suspect the canon went in for it too. Better not dig too deep: we have quite enough on our consciences already. Besides, as the pathetic old Socialists used to say, there's some murky secret at the beginning of every great estate: by what usury and violence did this house and the surrounding land come into the hands of the great family, whose debts brought them to ruin?"

"The eternal vicissitudes of families and peoples: in my opinion, nobody showed such a keen sense of it as Guicciardini, but in a gentle way; quite the opposite of our Verga, with his superstitions and fears," said the judge. He felt a sort of thirst to talk of books and writers, so rarely did he come across people with whom he could do so. And after looking at the Rosaspina engravings, he put down the book, and said: "Splendid: it won't have escaped Stendhal, with his love of Correggio."

"Surely not; and if he ever mentioned it in a letter or a note somewhere, Trompeo★ will know for sure . . . But the trouble with so many books printed by Bodoni is that when you try to read them you realise that the beauty of the printed page is worth much more than what it says. I have so many of them, but I think I've read only *Aminta* right through ... It's a shame: it would be splendid to read one's favourite books in a Bodoni edition".

"I have only one: Monti's *Aristodemo*."

"Beautiful, clear, but unreadable. And yet I like Monti, his contributions to the linguistic work of the Accademia della Crusca are a joy.★ And poor Monti, with his convoluted waltz-steps, gains by comparison with the things we've seen since the war, that I must confess I've been involved in too. You will have noticed my Fascist badge, at the hearings: I put it on out of ostentation. But the fact is, I am a party member. Do you know why, particularly? So they won't refuse me a passport."

From a door at the back of the room came a tall, dark young woman with very short hair, dressed in riding clothes like a Diana. "This is the lady who is living with me at present."

To the judge the sentence had an intriguingly detached and provisional ring, and while he was pondering the "at present", and, startled by the apparition, staring at her face full of cordiality and irony, he said almost inadvertently: "French."

"Yes, French," said the young lady, holding out her hand. "Of course, you guessed from my nose ... Oh Lord – the French nose!"

The judge blushed, because it was true. As he was articulating a clumsy compliment, his friend came to his rescue: "A lamb's hoof is the rather rustic expression for it in Sicily."

"An exact description, I'll remember it," she said. The talk went from noses to physiognomy and to Della Porta's★ book, which was taken down from a shelf. The judge felt a sense of repose and refreshment. And as he marvelled at the young lady's excellent Italian and her extensive knowledge of Italian writers and books, his friend explained: "Simone is *una francese italianizzante*, to Italianize one of their words. They form a sort of republic, as you well know, with Stendhal as First

Consul. They love what we most detest in ourselves. Think how Stendhal would have written up the wretched, sordid case we've been involved in ... the trouble with Italophiles, not only the French variety, is that they love the worst in us, and stop loving us as soon as they begin to see there is something better."

"Perhaps that's true," admitted Simone. "But I already know the best of this country, and I still love the Italians."

"It won't last," said her friend with a smile: but with a touch of melancholy, as if alluding to their relationship. "It's the same with all love. There's always some wrong assumption about the other. Just think of our love for any country not our own, and all the generalisations that leads to ... The Germans are thus and thus, the Spaniards, the French ... And what are Italians like? Not to mention Sicilians and all the hasty, dogmatic definitions made about them, judgements that allow no appeal ... All things considered, I think generalisations might work more or less by negatives: what we aren't, what we wouldn't want to be, and by implication what we would like to be, roughly speaking ... it would be amusing, and quite useful, to see European history in the guise of the Russians who would like to be Germans, Germans who'd like to be French, French who would like to be half German and half Italian while still remaining French, Spaniards who would settle for being English if they can't be Romans; and Italians who would like to be anything and everything except Italian ..."

"At this moment", said Simone, "all the Spaniards want to do is kill each other."

"With the moral support of Léon Blum," said the judge.

"Only moral to the party he's supposed to belong to," added Simone.

"Blum the socialist, Blum the Stendhalist: and what comes out of it but the masquerade of non-intervention," said their friend. "Mussolini sends telegrams congratulating Italian generals who conquer Spanish towns with Italian troops: and

Blum goes on talking calmly of non-intervention in Spain as if he believed in it . . ."

"Unless you accept that Mussolini has done so, nobody seems to realise that the war in Spain is the keystone of everything that is threatening the world," said the judge.

"And unless you accept again that Mussolini has realised it, with that buffoonery of his about the sword of Islam, while none of those directly involved have done so. It's the events in Tel Aviv that worry me," said his friend. "I often like to see history through some apparently insignificant detail, a shadowy figure, an anecdote . . . Napoleon goes into a synagogue, sees the Jews squatting at prayer, and tells them: 'Gentlemen, nobody has ever founded a state sitting down'; and now we've got bombs in the markets of Tel Aviv, an affair that will drag on for ever . . ."

This anxiety about news items relegated by the Spanish war to the small print, the terrorism of Jews wanting to found a State, and the way the English were handling their mandate in Palestine, seemed quite excessive to Simone and the judge, and bordering on the manic to turn it into a debating issue. However, their friend had travelled in the area, and seemed to know more about it than they did. So after a while that topic died away, and a cheerful, spirited discussion ensued about France, and about certain writers and books. And about Fascism. But when it was discussed in that way, Fascism seemed to recede, as if marked on an imaginary map of human folly.

It had been dark for a good while when the judge realised it was time, long past time, to go home. His friend (we can call him that now, from what we know came later) offered to take him in the car. Driving slowly, he talked about the woman who had come to live with him for a few months, as others had done in the past: ties that had left wonderful memories, partly because they had ended, as this one was destined to do. He talked of his travels. About his life in the country.

As they were saying goodbye, he said: "I felt a great admiration for you in the council chamber: you managed to pose the problem of the death penalty in the most terrible terms without ever referring to it directly."

"You too: I'm convinced that without your intervention the result ..."

"I only followed your lead. You've probably realised it already, but I wanted to tell you why I took part in the jury – to make a gesture against the death penalty ... Giolitti* said that no one in our country is refused a cigar and a mention on the honours list; nor yet a false medical certificate, I would add; I could have got one, too ..."

"I must admit I could have got out of this trial, too; in fact, I was advised to do so by someone in authority. But I saw it as a point of honour – of my whole life – of living."

"So we did it ... But how will it all end?"

"Badly," said the judge.

FIFTEEN

Since their conversation three months before, which he remembered as an ambiguous and painful one, the judge had often met the Prosecutor, but only in the corridors, where they would exchange a brief, almost reluctant nod. But meeting him in the corridor again after Christmas, and exchanging the usual sketchy greeting, the judge went on a few steps, and heard his name. He turned. "If you have half an hour to spare," said the Prosecutor, "come to my office for a chat." The tone was as cordial as the words.

"I am going to a hearing, but it shouldn't take long; I'll come, let's say in an hour."

"Splendid, I'll be waiting for you."

He went punctually. As if he did not recognise him the usher asked his name with some hauteur, then went in to announce him. Or perhaps he really hadn't recognised him and the hauteur was his usual way of protecting the Prosecutor from nuisance calls: but of late the judge had noticed many people behaving towards him like the usher.

The Prosecutor came to meet him at the door with an effusiveness that seemed to impress the usher. Instead of sitting at his desk and putting the judge the other side, he chose the two armchairs in a corner of the room with a round coffee-table in front of them, and an ash-tray on it. The Prosecutor pointed to it, saying: "Do smoke, if you like."

The judge was a little thrown by the reception.

"I hope," the Prosecutor began, "you didn't take amiss what I said to you some months ago. I must repeat that it was said with good-will and respect; as well as – I'm sure you realised at the time and now I can say so – out of – how can I put it? – a sort of professional concern: I didn't want any misunderstandings, friction, petty points of order, that might make for awkwardness between us, things being what they are – But it's all over now – Believe me, I don't feel the shadow of a reproach towards you, not in my heart of hearts; if I am to be perfectly frank, partly because the resentment has focused on you, and not upon the Palermo magistracy in general . . ."

"So I've noticed," said the judge.

"I'm sorry, believe me, very sorry: but that's how it is . . . Look: yesterday I received a copy of Lawyer Ungaro's protest to the Court of Cassation. I asked for it so that I could compare it with the one from our office: Ungaro is a great lawyer . . . Well, the verdict of the Assize Court in which you served is presented as the result of misguided scruples of conscience, and attributed to the distress and perplexity of the jury. The gravity of the penalty, it says, made them lose sight of the gravity of the crime, thus leading to a violation of the law and miscarriage of justice. You know I am in complete agreement with him: but I know, as everyone does, and perhaps he knows too, that the lay element, as he calls the jury, gave way to the opinion . . ."

"To my opinion, you mean . . . But they didn't give way at all: they already had what you call an opinion and I call principle. And the principle of opposition to capital punishent is so strong that you can feel quite sure you're in the right, even if you're alone in maintaining it – so I can't complain if people choose to believe that I convinced a reluctant jury by specious arguments against the death sentence . . . Only, to the credit of the jury, I can assure you that they were not reluctant."

"I'm glad," said the Prosecutor.

"Why?"

The Prosecutor hesitated, closed his eyes as if concentrating on his search for a reply. Then he seemed suddenly to crumple into weariness and old age, the network of wrinkles on his brow seemed closer and deeper, and he said: "I'm finishing in a few months; I'm leaving this office and this job. Retirement: a terrible prospect, why not admit it? for someone who has had the power I've had. But I'm adapting: I'm starting to think things I haven't thought till now. For example: that I have been a dead man who has buried other dead men. Furthermore: that that's what we all are, in this trade of accusing and judging. And then again: I wonder if, as dead men burying the dead, we really have the right to bury them by means of capital punishment. Don't misunderstand me: it's only a question, and I still think the answer is yes, we have the right, if the law requires it ... But when I told you just now that I am in complete agreement with Ungaro, as I said last time I was in complete agreement with Rocco, well, complete does not express what I really feel. There's something that disturbs me, and worries me, about affirming the law to that point ... On the threshold of old age, retirement, perhaps of death," his hand went to his chest, his fingers moved as if pressing something; it's angina, thought the judge, remembering his father, who died of it, making the same gesture; "I want to understand ... That's why I wanted to talk to you this morning, to understand what's happening to you now, what you feel, what you fear ... Not about your career, which you already know you have gambled away, and you knew from the first; but about your conscience, about life ..."

The judge would never have imagined a conversation with the Prosecutor turning into a confession, in fact, a plea for help. He said: "I'd be lying if I told you I felt quite calm."

"That's what I thought."

"I mean, I'm convinced I did my duty as a man and as a judge; I'm convinced I did my best, technically, with the legal arguments ... The chief argument for the defence should have been insanity; without it, I chose to adopt the tactic of including the three murders in one single criminal intention ...

Now I think with horror of what will happen ... What do I feel? Fear."

"I can tell you exactly what will happen: the Court of Cassation will annul your verdict, and assign the trial to the Assizes at Agrigento, where, I'm sorry to say, there's a President who has a weakness for the death penalty. There's also an old Socialist lawyer at Agrigento, I think he was once a deputy: a good lawyer and, needless to say, marked down as anti-Fascist. This lawyer will certainly take on the defence, which is all that's required to present this trial as a clash between Fascism, which comes down inexorably upon crimes of violence, and anti-Fascism with its squalid defence of them; which will no doubt have a secondary, retroactive effect on you and on your verdict. It will end with the death sentence, the defendant will be shot ... So, what will your verdict have achieved, except to prolong the agony?"

"*Ab uno disce omnes* ... I mean, knowing myself as I do, and presuming from this that I know other men, and this man in particular, I am almost certain that, condemned to imprisonment without hope, in the time that will elapse between the protests, the new trial, the death sentence and the appeal, he will manage to create a thread of hope for himself, however tenuous. Until the moment when they come and wake him one night to tell him the appeal has been rejected and that he will be shot before dawn, he will simply play out this thread, the more successfully if madness still comes to his aid. And from that moment, with the chaplain beside him, he will spend two or three terrible hours in agony, what we commonly refer to as the death-agony; that is, the feeling that life is over for him, that he'll never see the sun rise again, that he is about to cross the bounds of earthly night to enter into boundless night; not to mention all the terrible visions his mind will conjure up of the moment when death will explode in his body ..."

The Prosecutor mopped his brow, almost as if he were sweating in that chilly room.

"But agony, in the true sense of the word," the judge went on, "is really a state in which life has more part than death; so I will concede that the verdict has prolonged it for him. But it's like this: either this life of ours is just chance and absurdity, meaningful only in itself, in the illusions in which it is lived, falling short of any other illusion, and therefore living it a few more years, months or even days would seem to be a gift: just as it would to people suffering from cancer or tuberculosis, absurdly, in all its absurdity; or else our life is part of an inscrutable design, in which case the agony will serve to deliver this man up to some sort of hereafter with more thoughts, more reflection, perhaps with more madness, if not more faith."

"But all this, more thinking, more faith, as you say ... It's my feeling that it will come to him with an intensity no doubt more painful but at the same time – how can I say – more liberating, in the two or three hours when he knows he is about to go to his death."

"No, death is no longer a thought at that moment; indeed, there's nothing, at that moment, that can be called a thought. Try as you may, there's no way you can identify with it in the remotest degree."

"But don't you think you are finding an alibi for yourself, for the vanity, to be quite frank, of your protest within a context which allowed it only by heaping even greater suffering upon the human being upon whom you concentrated your defence of a principle; in short, that in defence of a principle you failed to take into account that man's suffering?"

"It's true that for me the defence of the principle counted for more than the life of the man. But it's a problem, not an alibi. I saved my soul, the jurors have saved theirs, which may all sound very convenient. But just think if every judge, one after another, were concerned to save his ..."

"It won't happen, you know that as well as I do."

"Yes, I know: and that's the counterpart, the horror and fear that I feel not just in connection with this trial ... But I'm consoled by this fantasy: that if all this, the world, life, our-selves, is nothing but someone's dream, as has been said, then this infinitesimal detail in his dream, the case we're discussing, the condemned man's agony, mine, yours, may yet serve to alert the dreamer that he is having nightmares, that he should turn over and try to have better dreams. At least, dreams without the death penalty."

"A fantasy," said the Prosecutor wearily. And then he stated wearily: "But you go on feeling horror, and fear."

"Yes."

"So do I. Of everything."

Notes

page **137** ARNOLD ZWEIG (1887–1968): German-Jewish author, socialist in outlook, exiled by the Nazis in 1934; *Der Streit um den Sergeanten Grischa* was published in 1928.

140 VITALIANO BRANCATI (1907–54): after initial attraction to Fascism, he turned away decisively in his novel *Gli anni perduti* (1935), and developed a satirical narrative style with specifically Sicilian themes, indirectly criticizing the Fascist regime in novels such as *Il Bell'Antonio*.

166 PAUL-LOUIS COURIER (1772–1825): pursued his classical studies while in French army in Italy, discovering a previously unknown Greek fragment in a Florentine library. The Biblioteca Laurenziana in Florence is chiefly important for its manuscript collection.

168 ARGISTO GIUFFREDI (c. 1535–93): wrote delicate Petrarchan verse and worked to promote the Tuscan dialect in Sicily. He held important offices when still a young man, fell into disfavour with certain ruling families, was excommunicated and imprisoned at Castellam-mare, where he died as the result of an explosion in the gunpowder depot.

168 CESARE BECCARIA (1738–94): author of *Dei delitti e delle pene* ("On crimes and punishments", 1764), in which he attacked capital punishment, torture and prison administrations. The book was widely read in its French translation (1766) and began a movement for penal reform in Western Europe.

169 GIUSEPPE PITRÈ (1841–1916): born in Palermo; a pioneer historian of popular culture, especially of Sicily. Published his model *Bibliografia delle tradizioni popolari in Italia* in 1894, and set up a Sicilian ethnographic museum in Palermo.

170 PHALARIS OF AKRAGAS: most famous of the Sicilian tyrants of the sixth century BC.

170 DIODORUS SICULUS: a Sicilian-Greek historian who wrote a world history in forty volumes c. 60–30 BC.

175 ALESSANDRO PAVOLINI: one-time secretary to Mussolini and Secretary of the newly constituted Partito Fascista Repubblicano (1943); captured in Mussolini's convoy in 1945 and executed along with fourteen others by the partisans.

179 ANDRÉ CHÉNIER: European symbol of the poet-hero, executed during the Terror: hero of Umberto Giordano's opera, *Andreas Chénier* (1896).

179 CAVARADOSSI: tragic hero of Puccini's *Tosca* – his lover, Tosca, thinks that she has obtained his safe-conduct and that his execution will be only a pretence.

190 CUORE (1886): famous sentimental children's book by Edmondo de Amicis.

190 PIETRO PAOLO TROMPEO: famous Italian scholar of French literature.

191 VINCENZO MONTI (1754–1828): Italian poet, remarkable for his political tergiversation. Translated the *Iliad*, wrote epics and tragedies including *Aristodemo*.

191 ACCADEMIA DELLA CRUSCA: formed by a group of scholars in the late sixteenth century to establish the supremacy of the Tuscan vernacular and oppose corruption of language, producing the *Vocabolario degli Accademici della Crusca* (1612). Monti led a Lombard school in opposition to this Tuscanism, and wrote a "Proposal for Some Corrections and Additions to The Crusca".

191 GIOVANNI BATTISTA DELLA PORTA (1543–1615): Neapolitan physicist and philosopher, wrote many comedies, also treatises on gardening, natural magic and *De humana phisiognomia* (1586).

194 GIOVANNI GIOLITTI (1842–1928): leading bourgeois liberal-democrat, five times prime minister, introduced universal suffrage. Initially tolerant of the Fascist government, but following the Matteoti crisis withdrew his support and spoke out against it.

Sciascia's Late Fiction

JOSEPH FARRELL

IT WAS A MATTER OF SOME SURPRISE when, late in his life, Leonardo Sciascia returned to fiction, and no one seemed more surprised than Sciascia himself. For some time, although his output had remained prolific, he had limited himself to works of a different type, including book-length interviews, books on aspects of Sicilian life, collections of essays and articles which had originally appeared in newspapers, as well as several works in that idiosyncratic genre which has no standard name, but which it will be convenient to tag "investigative essays". About half of his output falls into this category, and although it is common enough for writers to divide their time between fiction and non-fiction, the "investigative essay" was something Sciascia had made his own. None of his contemporaries produced anything in exactly that style, and his only precursor in the field was Alessandro Manzoni, the nineteenth-century novelist, whose pamphlet *The Column of Infamy*, denouncing and exposing the machinations of an Inquisition tribunal in Counter-Reformation Milan, provided Sciascia with a model and an inspiration.

Even if he takes an incident from history as his starting point, these investigative pieces of Sciascia's are not orthodox historical works. He generally preferred to use publicly available documents, and was more interested in analysis, comment and in observations, which could be arbitrary or whimsical, than in reconstruction. The approach is reminiscent of Borges – whose presence in Sciascia's writing became ever more marked – but where Borges would mix invention with fact, Sciascia would intertwine public event and private speculation. He revelled in the looseness of structure of his adopted genre and in the freedom it afforded him to roam at will through his material, intervening, speculating and, constantly, making an implicit contrast between, on the one hand, an order which could be given only by reason and, on the other, the disorder of history and the Machiavellian nature of human conduct. Perhaps the best-known work in this style was *The Moro Affair*, on the kidnapping and imprisonment of the ex-Christian Democrat Prime Minister by the Red Brigades. The work entitled *1912+1*, published in 1986, is of the same type. In it Sciascia recounts the known facts of a celebrated murder case in the decadent high society of pre-World War I Italy, when King Umberto was monarch of the nation and Gabriele D'Annunzio monarch of letters. D'Annunzio worshipped the Nietzschean superman, that ambiguous figure who, in his dealings with other men – or women – viewed himself as exempt from the laws of all conventional morality (or "the code of the slave"). His novels are impregnated with a Swinburnean sensuality, and Sciascia, in addition to exposing what to him seemed an evident injustice in the case in question, explored the links between the D'Annunzian culture of the time and the actual conduct of men and women.

According to his own account (in a conversation in Syracuse), when he sat down with the documents he had accumulated on another murder case in Palermo during the years of Fascism, he had every intention of writing the same kind of book. Sciascia followed a fixed routine, collecting his material in winter and writing over the summer months. He insisted that he never thought in advance about form, and that he never found it necessary to rewrite. *Open Doors* only became a novel once he started to write. It was published in 1987 and was his first work of fiction since *Candido* ten years previously. It also represented a return to the detective story, the form he had used for his first four novels but had abandoned after *One Way or Another* in 1974. He subsequently produced the two other detective stories contained in this volume: *The*

Knight and Death the following year, and *A Straightforward Tale* in 1989, a few months before his death in November of the same year.

Since the return to fiction was haphazard, there is little point in attempting to build an ideology into it, but it is intriguing to note the extent to which in his last novels Sciascia re-covers old ground, re-examines familiar topics, analyses again the themes which have always obsessed him, but from a different perspective. It was always facile to view Sciascia exclusively as a survivor from the Age of the Enlightenment, as the upholder of the concept of Law in a land which despised it, as the solitary hero engaged on quest for Justice and Truth, or the intrepid adversary of violence and mafia in Sicily. Gore Vidal pointed out that from his Sicilian experience Sciascia forged something unique which spoke to all European peoples, and it seems clear that, in his last novels, he was attempting to widen his canvas. to use his subject matter as metaphor. He remains close to history, and as he again recounts episodes associated with Fascism, terrorism and mafia, there is at times a real tension between history and metaphor. These had been familiar topics in his principal works, but here life itself is seen by an old man, who knew he was dying. At times, in these books, the world seems to be glimpsed through a hospital window, and nothing is more moving and striking than the cosmic pity and compassion with which these novels are imbued. Sciascia had not been a notably compassionate writer at other times, but all his life he shadowed his fellow Sicilian, Luigi Pirandello. In the nihilistic world-view Pirandello adhered to – most forcibly expressed in his essay *On Humour* – a sense of compassion for the ultimate plight of the human being was the one positive, life-enhancing value which survived. It is this quality which emerges most tellingly in Sciascia's final phase.

Fascism, terrorism and mafia intrigue feature in the three final novels. *Open Doors* is set in the Fascist period, as had been the first of his writings, *The Parishes of Regalpetra*. He was always contemptuous both of Mussolini's Fascism as well as of what he judged "the eternal Italian fascism", and many of the characters in his works are presented as coming to maturity at the moment they free themselves from it. *The Knight and Death* has evident links, both thematic and stylistic, with the sinister, tangled political society depicted in *Equal Danger*, while the posthumous *Straightforward Tale* can be seen as return to, and an updating of the mafia world of his first novel, *Day of the Owl*.

Although *Open Doors* is set in 1937, the Fascist period, by openly introducing references to the year of writing, 1987, Sciascia introduces an element of movement between fictional and real time. There is no demand for the "willing suspension of disbelief", but there are few of the other customary attributes or features of traditional fiction. This work is half-way between the novel and the "investigative essay" of the sort Sciascia had in mind when he started writing, but in form and approach it is also in line with novels produced by such contemporary writers as Kundera and Vargas Llosa. The leading character is in reality Sciascia himself. It is odd that at the moment when the pundits of post-modernist criticism have declared the author dead, novelists have made themselves more visible than at any preceding time. Discussing the "little judge" whom he had apparently created, Sciascia suddenly announces that when he had seen him in life, he was not in fact "little" at all, at least not in stature, but that in some imprecise way he had made an impression of littleness on Sciascia. This physical "littleness", Sciascia explains, was a mere invention to emphasise his moral and human grandeur. At times, Sciascia puts his reflections into the mouth of one of the characters, but just as frequently he talks in prima persona.

Sciascia was never strong on description, and at no time in this novel does he spend a word in recreating period atmosphere or providing any kind of physical background. He never provides any description of his characters, apart from a few somewhat cloying, florid words on the women. His fictional world is a purely intellectual construct, inhabited by intellectuals. The characters are given no names. None of them have any life outside what is strictly required for the development of the central conflict. They have no emotional life, in the sense of affections, friendships, sexual relations. They are cyphers, or creations drawn, like Cubist sketches, on a deliberately flat surface. Anonymity is preferred, perhaps because anonymity crushes individuality. In the Book of Genesis, names are given to creatures so that they can be distinguished one from the other.

Is it then possible to arrive at some understanding of what fiction was for Sciascia? Years previously he accused himself of not having a "great creative imagination", adding that for his characters, unlike those of Pirandello, "the distance between life and the printed page is minimal, the gap very slight." Fiction in Sciascia is not creation *ex nihilo*, nor is it the manufacture of a parallel world. He never was a writer who set out to create an alternative universe, where the rules of physics, of time and space relationships could be suspended at will. Unlike the South American exponents of magical realism such as Marquez, he never had the inclination to rebel against existing conditions by allowing his fantasy to manufacture a dimension where recognisable and purely invented elements become one. He adhered to certain conventions. It is not too much to say that his creativity is essentially realistic, yet in these novels he strains at the leash.

The novella *A Straightforward Tale* is the most evidently realist of his later works. The title is clearly ironic, and if it does not have the multi-layered richness of the other stories, it is a masterly exercise in narrative. Indeed, it is as expertly plotted as any work of Sciascia's. On this occasion there is no temptation to go beyond the conventional bounds of the novel into territory more usually assigned to the essay. The land is Sicily, the characters Sicilian, and the villains are, although the word is never used, the modern mafia of drug-dealers. Behind them lurks that complex network of corruption and double dealing involving Church and police which makes this tale a *tour de force* of detective fiction, and of life in Sicily such a nightmare. The reality depicted is anything but straightforward.

The strength of Sciascia's fictional world comes from the power of the intellect which created it, from the decency (in the sense Orwell attached to the word) of the values advocated rather than from the richness of imagination called into play. More and more the two styles of his books came closer together. It would be curious to know if he would have written *Open Doors* differently if he had adhered to his original intention of presenting it as an investigative essay. Perhaps it is only a novel because he says it is. In it, Sciascia is engaged on a quest, and it is not a search for the inner life of individual characters, but a quest for public values. He unites in a unique way a relativism over fact reminiscent of Borges or Pirandello with a moral absolutism which is as rigid as any Counter-Reformation Jesuit would have wished. As a writer, he proclaims the need to stand by a notion of the value of a truth which at first sight finds no response in his own sceptical treatment of history. The truth in question is, of course, moral truth.

In *Open Doors* the facts of the case are provided by history, but they are briefly, even cursorily and contemptuously, reported inside a framework of debate and discussion. The novel opens with a discussion between the two legal figures over the prospect of actually imposing the recently re-introduced death penalty and closes with a discussion between the same two characters over the value of the outcome of the case in the court of first instance. The Prosecution will undoubtedly appeal against the decision not to apply the death penalty. There is only one other extended dialogue in the work, between the judge and the farmer, and that, unsurprisingly in Sciascia, concerns bookish matters. The three murders committed by the "Beast" are given in a rapid journalistic summary, but only when Sciascia is almost half-way through his tale. Information about the presumably anxious debates in the jury room is conveyed in one para-graph which is so restrained and spare as to be almost laugh-able. Considering the nature of the crimes, anything further from what John Buchan would have called a "shocker" is hard to imagine.

The central fact is not the crime, but the potential punish-ment: the death penalty. The focus of Sciascia's attention has shifted on to the criminal, but only in as much as the criminal can be in his own way a victim. The Accused, the Beast – and the enormity of his crime or the fact of his guilt is never in dispute – is by now a captive, a prisoner, a human being who might well be torn apart by the machine. Whatever his tena-ciously held abstract position on Law and Justice founded on Reason, Sciascia never can bring himself to regard the actual judicial machinery with any tenderness. He was too much of a Sicilian to regard the judge charged with discharging the law with anything other than uncomprehending distaste, or to regard the living human being who faces the rigours of the law with anything other than fellow feeling. In some ways, the Accused is in the same position as Aldo Moro, or of those of Sciascia's heroes who face death or pain at the hands of the Inquisition, of terrorists, of the mafia, or of any tyrannical force which has arrogated to itself the power of God over the destinies of other humans. There is in this complex standpoint a mixture of an attitude born of centuries of Sicilian history, and of a more universal, liberal distaste for the taking of life whatever the circumstances.

Fascism had always been the very synonym for the forces of unreason, the antithesis of any life-enhancing value, or even of Life. In this work, the metaphorical sense of Fascism is as significant as the strictly historical. Fascism re-introduced the death penalty, but Fascism itself is a death force. All that counts against it is the commitment of the individual, but plainly that commitment is doomed to failure. The splendid closing dialogue between the two lawyers, by now reconciled on a human level, is a discussion of how to confront and cope with the inevitability of defeat. The Prosecutor believes that the judge had wasted his time in opposing the death penalty, not so much because the sentence will undoubtedly be over-turned on appeal as because the decision will merely expose the guilty man to an extended period of anxiety and a longer period of futile hope. Against this, the judge urges that all life is transient, that no hope is ever futile, that the individual in whatever desperate circumstances will invariably find consolation in even the most illusory of hopes and that ultimately the principle of the final, intrinsic value of life itself must be asserted always and everywhere – against the forces of death.

Figurative elements become the determinant, essential element of the style and approach in *The Knight and Death*. The novel is a meditation, infused with elements of poetry, on life and death. The theatre of action is presumably Rome, but the city is given no name and it is part of a Kafkaesque planet from which all coherence has fled. Sciascia operates here on the verges of history, for if the terrorist-dominated society is not entirely unfamiliar from recent Italian experience, the division between terrorist activity and legitimate government action is blurred. It is no longer clear where power resides, any more than it was to K, but it is a sinister force which can construct an opposition as shady as itself, and which can destroy capriciously. Society is a moral quagmire, where the idealistic preach slaughter, where the weak-minded execute these teachings out of a desire for status, excitement and acceptance, while behind them lurk cynical, grey men who manipulate both groups, drawing from the anarchy they have unleashed comfort and justification for their own domination. The authoritarianism of established power of whatever hue – old divisions into Right and Left have lost all sense – bases itself on the disorder it has itself created. In this labyrinthine world, Machiavelli and the mafia blend. Principles are matters for public consumption but there is never any savour of them in practice.

The print which gives the novel its title was the property of the Deputy who once again is given no individual name. The theme is a reprise of the topics Sciascia had developed in an earlier novel *Equal Danger*, and if he subtitled that novel a "parody", he subtitles this later work a "sotie". A sotie is defined as a satirical farce from the fifteenth and sixteenth centuries, but it was adopted by André Gide as a description of *The Vatican Cellars*. The term *sotie* does not suggest, any more than the term parody, that Sciascia was intending to write what Graham Greene dubbed an Entertainment. Nor is it a pastiche, although that term has now acquired more respectable connotations in certain critical circles. Sciascia's purposes were always fundamentally serious. It would be flippant and otiose to attach x=y type equations to the three figures from the engraving, but the sense of death hangs over the book, and the devil is, in a purely humanistic sense, required as the counterpoint to forces which wish to present themselves as the forces of good and right. The battlefield for this modern Pilgrim's Progress is of course politics, but the action is seen from the perspective of a man who knows he is dying.

In some ways this is a work which is as much put together from pre-existing sources as Umberto Eco's *The Name of the Rose*. For those with a taste for such matters, the novel is a thicket of what are now called intertextual references. The images from Dürer's etching haunt the Deputy's mind, but the identical print was in the possession of another celebrated fictional detective, Inspector Barlach of the Berne police, and was used by his creator Friedrich Dürrenmatt for the same purposes in *The Judge And The Executioner*. Similarly, Sciascia pays homage to the greatest of all Italian detective stories, C. E. Gadda's *That Awful Mess On Via Merulana*, by introducing references to its hero, Inspector Ciccio Ingravallo. He is equally generous to R. L. Stevenson's *Treasure Island* and quotes copiously from writers ranging from Feydeau to D. H. Lawrence. Hand in hand with these references to literary antecedents go a series of throwaway remarks which imply that the whole plot was a joke. The initial encounter between Aurispa and Sandoz at the banquet before the murder was intended, according to Aurispa, as a joke. The young man who is arrested after making the telephone call in which he passed himself off as a terrorist protests that he was only playing a joke, leading the Deputy to conclude that "we are inside a sotie."

These references both shadow and shape the development of the action. They are neither intellectually clever exercises in counterpoint, nor do they signify that the novel is intended as no more than a purely literary construct. They are something of both, as the novel itself is much more. The "artificial" nature of the novel, its tendency to keep history at arm's length, to see the events of the book through a prism reflects the very nature of the events recounted. As is invariably the case with Sciascia's detective stories, the case is not solved inside the confines of the novel, but the reader will have no doubt of who is responsible. The dilemma is resolved by reference to a wise man – in this case Dr Rieti, who had followed the affairs of the two rival industrialists but who himself will end up a victim of murder squads for talking to the Deputy. The final victim is the Deputy, killed by some unknown group who could be the Children of Eighty-nine, by this time brought into existence. Death is the only victor.

Whatever the truth about Power and the Children of Eighty-nine – this is Pirandellian territory where illusion and reality overlap – the world is ruled by a system of self-perpetuating corruption. All power is ultimately mafioso in its operations, but not all activities can be covert. A devil of some sort is essential. If the old-style devil is no longer serviceable, a newer model must be summoned up, and fortunately there are always enough weak-minded individuals prepared to offer themselves for the task in return for fifteen minutes' celebrity. The self-proclaimed activist in the Saint Just cell serves the purpose here. The police leap on both the man and this confirmation that their work was on the right lines. His arrest proves that all is right with the world, that the old order was fundamentally sound – precisely the standard ending of the classical detective story. No doubt the wrong man has been – almost certainly – unmasked, but he can act as a very modern devil, allowing real evil to continue unchecked.

As always, the detective protagonist is a highly cultured intellectual, and at a certain point Sciascia seems to lose interest in his plot and to turn to the dilemma and character of the Deputy himself. The last sections – from his quitting the police station on temporary leave until his murder – provide prose of the most refined, limpid and perspicacious order. At times, Sciascia attains that level of meditative prose which is the distinctive quality of the supreme essayist, and this passage, where the Deputy reaches the "threshold of prayer", displays a quality of mercy, a measure of open-hearted benignity towards humankind worthy of Montaigne. Like Sciascia, the Deputy knew he was dying, but his dying was not embittered by hatred for life. Death itself may be the ultimate absurdity, but Sciascia never reaches the point of believing that the absurdity of death makes the living that precedes it senseless and vain. The central drawback of modern criticism is that in concentrating on scientific or linguistic aspects, it loses sight of the quest for and assertion of values which are as intrinsic to certain works of literature as they are fundamental to life. To overlook that feature of quest and assertion in Sciascia is to diminish him.

LEONARDO SCIASCIA

"During the last quarter century, Sciascia has made out of his curious Sicilian experience a literature that is not quite like anything else ever done by a European"

GORE VIDAL, *New York Review of Books*

Sicilian Uncles

The Day of the Owl

Equal Danger

The Wine-Dark Sea

One Way or Another

The Mystery of Majorana

The Moro Affair

FORTHCOMING

The Council of Egypt

Death of an Inquisitor

Candido or A Dream dreamed in Sicily

Harvill Paperbacks are published by Harvill, an Imprint of HarperCollins*Publishers*

1. Giuseppe Tomasi di Lampedusa *The Leopard*
2. Boris Pasternak *Doctor Zhivago*
3. Alexander Solzhenitsyn *The Gulag Archipelago 1918–1956*
4. Jonathan Raban *Soft City*
5. Alan Ross *Blindfold Games*
6. Joy Adamson *Queen of Shaba*
7. Vasily Grossman *Forever Flowing*
8. Peter Levi *The Frontiers of Paradise*
9. Ernst Pawel *The Nightmare of Reason*
10. Patrick O'Brian *Joseph Banks*
11. Mikhail Bulgakov *The Master and Margarita*
12. Leonid Borodin *Partings*
13. Salvator Satta *The Day of Judgement*
14. Peter Matthiessen *At Play in the Fields of the Lord*
15. Alexander Solzhenitsyn *The First Circle*
16. Homer, translated by Robert Fitzgerald *The Odyssey*
17. George MacDonald Fraser *The Steel Bonnets*
18. Peter Matthiessen *The Cloud Forest*
19. Theodore Zeldin *The French*
20. Georges Perec *Life A User's Manual*
21. Nicholas Gage *Eleni*
22. Eugenia Ginzburg *Into the Whirlwind*
23. Eugenia Ginzburg *Within the Whirlwind*
24. Mikhail Bulgakov *The Heart of a Dog*
25. Vincent Cronin *Louis and Antoinette*
26. Alan Ross *The Bandit on the Billiard Table*
27. Fyodor Dostoyevsky *The Double*
28. Alan Ross *Time Was Away*
29. Peter Matthiessen *Under the Mountain Wall*
30. Peter Matthiessen *The Snow Leopard*
31. Peter Matthiessen *Far Tortuga*
32. Jorge Amado *Shepherds of the Night*
33. Jorge Amado *The Violent Land*
34. Jorge Amado *Tent of Miracles*
35. Torgny Lindgren *Bathsheba*
36. Antæus *Journals, Notebooks & Diaries*
37. Edmonde Charles-Roux *Chanel*
38. Nadezhda Mandelstam *Hope Against Hope*
39. Nadezhda Mandelstam *Hope Abandoned*
40. Raymond Carver *Elephant and Other Stories*
41. Vincent Cronin *Catherine, Empress of All the Russias*
42. Federico de Roberto *The Viceroys*
43. Yashar Kemal *The Wind from the Plain*
44. Yashar Kemal *Iron Earth, Copper Sky*

45. Yashar Kemal *The Undying Grass*
46. Georges Perec *W or the Memory of Childhood*
47. Antæus *On Nature*
48. Roy Fuller *The Strange and the Good*
49. Anna Akhmatova *Selected Poems*
50. Mikhail Bulgakov *The White Guard*
51. Lydia Chukovskaya *Sofia Petrovna*
52. Alan Ross *Coastwise Lights*
53. Boris Pasternak *Poems 1955–1959* and *An Essay in Autobiography*
54. Marta Morazzoni *Girl in a Turban*
55. Eduardo Mendoza *City of Marvels*
56. Michael O'Neill *The Stripped Bed*
57. Antæus *Literature as Pleasure*
58. Margarete Buber-Neumann *Milena*
59. Torgny Lindgren *Merab's Beauty*
60. Jaan Kaplinski *The Same Sea in Us All*
61. Mikhail Bulgakov *A Country Doctor's Notebook*
62. Vincent Cronin *Louis XIV*
63. David Gilmour *The Last Leopard*
64. Leo Perutz *The Marquis of Bolibar*
65. Claudio Magris *Danube*
66. Jorge Amado *Home is the Sailor*
67. Richard Ford *Wildlife*
68. Alexander Solzhenitsyn *One Day in the Life of Ivan Denisovich*
69. Andrei Bitov *Puskin House*
70. Yashar Kemal *Memed, My Hawk*
71. Raymond Carver *A New Path to the Waterfall*
72. Peter Matthiessen *On the River Styx*
73. Ernst Pawel *The Labyrinth of Exile*
74. John Clive *Not By Fact Alone*
75. Osip Mandelstam *Stone*
76. Elias Khoury *Little Mountain*
77. Osip Mandelstam *The Collected Critical Prose and Letters*
78. Edward Hoagland *Heart's Desire*
79. Mikhail Bulgakov *Black Snow*
80. Evgeny Pasternak *Boris Pasternak: The Tragic Years 1930–60*
81. Leonid Borodin *The Third Truth*
82. Michael Hulse *Eating Strawberries in the Necropolis*
83. Antæus *Jubilee Edition*
84. Robert Hughes *Nothing If Not Critical*
85. Alexander Solzhenitsyn *Rebuilding Russia*
86. Yury Dombrovsky *The Keeper of Antiquities*
87. Mikhail Bulgakov *Diaboliad*
88. Penelope Fitzgerald *The Knox Brothers*
89. Oleg Chukhontsev *Dissonant Voices: The New Russian Fiction*
90. Peter Levi *The Hill of Kronos*
91. Henry Green *Living*
92. Gesualdo Bufalino *Night's Lies*

93. Peter Matthiessen *Partisans*
94. Georges Perec *Things / A Man Asleep*
95. C. K. Stead *The Death of the Body*
96. Leo Perutz *By Night under the Stone Bridge*
97. Henry Green *Caught*
98. Lars Gustafsson *The Death of a Beekeeper*
99. Ismail Kadare *Broken April*
100. Peter Matthiessen *In the Spirit of Crazy Horse*
101. Yashar Kemal *To Crush the Serpent*
102. Elspeth Huxley *Nine Faces of Kenya*
103. Jacques Presser *The Night of the Girondists*
104. Julien Gracq *A Balcony in the Forest*
105. Henry Green *Loving*
106. Jaan Kaplinski *The Wandering Border*
107. William Watson *The Last of the Templars*
108. Penelope Fitzgerald *Charlotte Mew and Her Friends*
109. George MacDonald Fraser *Mr American*
110. Gustaw Herling *The Island*
111. Marguerite Yourcenar *Anna, Soror . . .*
112. Dominic Cooper *Men at Axlir*
113. Vincent Cronin *The Golden Honeycomb*
114. Aleksandr Kushner *Apollo in the Snow*
115. Antæus *Plays in One Act*
116. Vasily Grossman *Life and Fate*
117. Mikhail Bulgakov *Manuscripts Don't Burn*
118. C. K. Stead *Sister Hollywood*
119. José Saramago *The Year of the Death of Ricardo Reis*
120. Gesualdo Bufalino *Blind Argus*
121. Peter Matthiessen *African Silences*
122. Leonid Borodin *The Story of a Strange Time*
123. Raymond Carver *No Heroics, Please*
124. Jean Strouse *Alice James*
125. Javier Marías *All Souls*
126. Henry Green *Nothing*
127. Marguerite Yourcenar *Coup de Grâce*
128. Patrick Modiano *Honeymoon*
129. Georges Perec *"53 Days"*
130. Ferdinand Mount (ed.) *Communism*
131. John Gross (ed.) *The Modern Movement*
132. Leonardo Sciascia *The Knight and Death*
133. Leopard 2
134. Leo Perutz *Little Apple*